D1145171

First published 2022 by Two Hoots, an imprint of Pan Macmillan
The Smithson, 6 Briset Street, London EC1M 5NR
EU representative: Macmillan Publishers Ireland Limited, 1st Floor, The Liffey Trust Centre,
117-126 Sheriff Street Upper, Dublin 1, D01 YC43

Associated companies throughout the world
www.panmacmillan.com
ISBN 978-1-5290-7150-4
Introduction and selection copyright © Dapo Adeola 2022

Foreword Text © Patrice Lawrence 2022, illustrations © Dapo Adeola 2022
'The South Crong Bake-Off' Text © Alex Wheatle 2022, illustrations © Arantza Peña Popo 2022
'Good Reception' Text © Sharna Jackson 2022, illustrations © Olu Oke 2022
'Who Said Summer Was Fun?' Text © Yasmin Joseph 2022, illustrations © Denzell Dankwah 2022
'My Body Knows Beats' Text © Zaïre Krieger 2022, illustrations © Ashley Evans 2022
'Lost and Found' Text © Kelechi Okafor 2022, illustrations © Dorcas Magbadelo 2022
'Sunshine Girl' Text © Camryn Garrett 2022, illustrations © Charis JB 2022
'Sticks and Stones' Text © Koleka Putuma 2022, illustrations © Snalo Ngcaba 2022
'Halloween Dance' Text © Funmbi Omotayo 2022, illustrations © Michael Kennedy 2022
'Family is Family' Text © Doreen Baingana 2022, illustrations © Camilla Sucre 2022
'Into the Future' Text © Jeffrey Boakye 2022, illustrations © Tomekah George 2022
'Ancestral Voices' Text © Trish Cooke 2022, illustrations © Rahana Dariah 2022
'Nigerian Jollof' Text and illustrations © Dapo Adeola 2022
'Nan's Jollof Rice' Text © Rosaline Tella 2022, illustrations © Dapo Adeola 2022
'The Way Home' Text © Maame Blue 2022, illustrations © Robyn Smith 2022
'The Book of You' Text © Dorothy Koomson 2022, illustrations © Awuradwoa Afful 2022
'Best Laid Plans' Text © Tracey Baptiste 2022, illustrations © Lewis James 2022
'Sting Like a Butterfly' Text © Faridah Àbíké-Íyímídé 2022, illustrations © Kofi Ofosu 2022
'Chasing Joy' Text © Hannah Lee 2022, illustrations © Ken Wilson-Max 2022
'Plantain Moi Moi' Text © Adejoké 'Joké' Bakare 2022, illustrations © Ojima Abalaka 2022
'Webjørn's Song' Text © Nathan Bryon 2022, illustrations © Jess Nash 2022
'The Skin I'm In' Text © Malorie Blackman 2022, illustrations © Odera Igbokwe 2022
'The Owner of the Story' Text © Matilda Feyiṣayọ Ibini 2022, illustrations © Terrence Adegbenle 2022

Moral rights asserted.

Pan Macmillan does not have any control over, or any responsibility for, any author or third
party websites referred to in or on this book.

9 8 7 6 5 4 3 2 1
A CIP catalogue record for this book is available from the British Library.
Printed in Italy

www.twohootsbooks.com

Stories Celebrating Black Voices

Curated by Dapo Adeola

TWO HOOTS

CONTENTS

FOREWORD

PATRICE LAWRENCE

In the last two years, I have almost managed to convince myself that there is no joy in the world. Even this morning, when I turn on the news, I imagine Happiness bundling their belongings into a spotted handkerchief and tying it onto a stick that they sling over their shoulder. They don't want to go, but my imagination is pushing them through that wardrobe door to a different world where they feel more welcome. As I'm about to shut them out, they shove their foot between the door.

'Come on, hun,' they say. 'Don't send me away. The world is a bit grim, but you absolutely know there's joy around.' Then they put a hand over their mouth as if hiding a smile and add, 'I know because I've seen you dancing to K-Pop when you think no one's looking. You seem pretty happy then!'

And Happiness is right (not about Korean pop music. It's Korean indie music that I flick a quick shimmy to while I'm loading the dishwasher). Joy is throwing out moves all around us. Sometimes it's a big electric slide of joy, where we're all joined together in the same moment, grinning. Did you watch the Tokyo Olympics women's skateboarding final? I was messaging with friends about the awesome skill and courage of the skateboarders, but it was the young women's kindness and support towards each other that gave me joy.

Sometimes, joy feels like a flash mob performance. A solitary musician sits on a bench and plays a few notes. Everyone walks past. Then another musician joins her and then another. Suddenly, there's that glorious pull in the heart of something familiar and uplifting. Or joy might just be like that solo musician, quiet, understated and beautiful.

Often, though, joy has felt out of my sight. Perhaps it's like the ballet dancer, Misty Copeland, performing the ultimate pirouette of perfection but my back is turned away so I can't see her. I often feel despair and helplessness at the challenges faced by Black people across the world. Of course, moments of joy still weave through my life, but I need someone to show me where to look.

This is why *Joyful, Joyful* is so important. Black writers from around the world are reminding us of the power of love, community and kindness. Black artists make our imaginations sing as characters dance off the page – and some of them sting like a butterfly too! Yes, there is sadness, fear and uncertainty, but this anthology hums with hope and virtually whistles with words that will make us grin. Think of it as your own portable flash mob of happiness, as page by page, your heart lifts and you are joyful, joyful too.

Introduction

DAPO ADEOLA

When I first started illustrating books back in 2018, I was shocked to find out that aside from myself who was yet to be published, I only knew of one other Black British illustrator working on the scene at the time. I set about trying to find out if, as I believed, there were more talents out there in the community waiting to be discovered. The search gave me the idea for this anthology back in 2019.

My goal was to offer an opportunity for the joyful and different voices and stories within the Black diaspora to be heard by members of the same diaspora, as well as people from other backgrounds. I wanted to create something that I wish had been available to me as a young reader when I was growing up. A book that allowed me to see myself and others reflected in stories that speak about more than just our struggle, stories that tell of our joy, imagination and creativity.

As my confidence grew, so too did the concept, to the point where it's become this beautiful, colourful and multi-layered book of discovery and wonder that gives an insight into how rich our storytelling talents are within the global Black diaspora. To say I'm proud of what we've put together here would be an understatement.

We hope that you enjoy reading and sharing these joyful stories as much as, if not more than we've enjoyed creating them for you. Maybe you will want to share your own story, too.

The South Crong Bake-Off

ALEX WHEATLE
ARANTZA PEÑA POPO

Ten minutes to go till school was done for the day. *I must disappear from this class and ding Dad.*

I raised a hand.

'Yes, McKay, what is it?' Ms Chin-Loy asked.

'Miss, I really need to use the gents,' I said.

Ms Chin-Loy checked her watch and side-eyed me. 'There are only nine minutes until the end of my lesson. Can't you hold on until then?'

'I've gotta go, Miss. I'm bursting. If I stay in my seat it's gonna get damp.'

'He's lying,' Kiran Cassidy shouted. 'He just wants to get out of class early! Don't let him play you, Miss.'

I glared at Kiran. Ms Chin-Loy placed her hands on her hips and thought about it. 'OK, if you must go, go.'

I rolled out of that classroom like a polo-bear on a ski slope. When I reached the boys' toilets, I dinged Dad.

'Have you got my ingredients?' I asked. 'Including the sugar?'

'Everything you asked for, I've bought,' Dad confirmed. 'Even a small flask of Jamaican rum. *Only* for baking purposes.'

'Thanks, Dad.'

'I'll be outside the gates in five minutes,'

'Dad,' I replied. 'I'm gonna win this thing. Trust me on that.'

'It's not all about winning, McKay.'

Dad was wrong. I made a bet with Liccle Bit. If I won, he'd have to sketch a portrait of me and put it in a neat frame, and if I lost, I'd have to cook him his fave meal of lamb shanks and baby potatoes. Lamb shanks are proper expensive.

It was serious.

I killed the call, washed my hands and hot-toed back to class.

I'm gonna blast this competition. Been practising my rum, mango and apple crumble for weeks. I used to cook it with Mum. If Ms Penn doesn't give me that golden apron and the fifty pounds of book tokens, then something's wrong with the world.

Half past three licked and I foot-slapped to the school gates. Dad handed over the shopping bag of ingredients and I took a quick look inside.

'Thanks, Dad.'

'Good luck but respect your competitors,' he said. 'I'm off to work and *don't* stay up too late.'

'Stay up late? Me? As if I'd ever.'

Dad half-grinned. 'Do your mum proud,' he said as he stepped away.

'I will.'

I spotted Saira and Venetia on the way to the Food Tech classroom.

'You're not coming to watch?' I asked. 'It's the South Crong Bake-Off. You're my cheerleaders and I want some big McKay love.'

'Cheerleaders?' repeated Venetia. 'If you're lucky you might hear one clap from us but only if whatever you're baking doesn't flop.'

'You'll be on time?' I fretted.

'Of course,' Saira said. 'Just going home to change. They're letting people in at four thirty, right?'

'Yep, that's right. You don't wanna miss this. It's gonna be epic. You'll be telling your grandchildren that you were there when I made my legendary super-duper crumble. One day, there'll be a statue of it outside Crong Town Hall. Trust me on that!'

* * *

Ms Penn stood outside the Food Tech classroom wearing her long African print dress and a gold head-wrap. Gold earrings niced up her lobes and silver bangles decorated her wrists. 'Happy you made it, McKay. Everybody's here. Go and find yourself a spot.'

Alan Gilzean was there. Precious Murphy, Idolyn Cooper and Samantha Watson too. They all placed their ingredients on the counters. They all looked like this was the most serious thing they had to do in their whole life. They weren't wrong. Tension hot-rushed through my arteries.

Dad had packed Mum's old apron into the shopping bag. I took it out and tied it on. Pride filled me. I emptied out my items.

Plain flour, digestive biscuits, butter, porridge oats, apple juice, orange juice. Granulated brown sugar.

Oh no! Macaroni in a puddle! It's meant to be soft *brown sugar.*

'Ms Penn!' I almost screamed. 'Ms Penn!'

She came over. 'Keep your voice down, McKay.'

'My dad got me granulated brown sugar!' I panicked. 'Gotta flash-foot outta here and get some soft brown sugar.'

Ms Penn checked her watch. 'We open the doors at four thirty. Make sure you're back ten minutes before then. If not, we'll have to start without you.'

I was outta the classroom on the 't' of 'then'. *Dagthorn's store in the middle of the estate – he might have some soft brown sugar. He better have it.*

By the time I reached the shop I must've lost five pounds. Mr Dagthorn's daughter, Juniper, was at the till. She admired her nails. Today, her hair was electric-shock blue.

'Juniper!' I gasped. 'Got any soft brown sugar? For baking?'

Juniper thought about it and shook her head.

'We only got white sugar.'

'Can you check?' I pleaded.

'No need to check,' Juniper said. 'My dad never stocks brown sugar. You're gonna have to bounce to the supermarket.'

'You can't be telling me this!'

'I'm telling you this.'

Juniper went back to studying her shiny black nails.

I checked the time on my phone. 3:41 p.m.

What do I do? What do I do? The supermarket is at least a twenty-minute trod. And I'm tired already.

I stepped out of the shop.

Who's that on the motorised scooter? Morgan Stapleton, the mad afro boy in my English class.

'Morgan!' I yelled. 'Moooorgaaaaan!' He turned around and wheeled towards me.

'I need your *scooter*. It's an emergency. A matter of precious life and serious death!'

Morgan looked me up and down. 'Your weight will concave it, bruv.'

'No, it won't,' I argued. 'I'll rent it off you.'

'How much you got?' Morgan asked.

I searched my pockets. 'Two pounds fifty-eight pence.'

'All right,' Morgan nodded. 'But if you buckle it, mash it or dent it then you have to buy me a Mercedes one.'

Is that a thing? Do Mercedes make scooters?

'Yes, yes, yes,' I agreed, got on and hot-wheeled away.

I Lewis Hamiltoned to the supermarket, not slowing down when I busted the corners.

Picked up the soft brown sugar.

Oh no! There was a queue at the self check-out!

This can't be happening.

A till was vacated and I hot-toed towards it. People tut-tutted behind me, but I didn't care. *There's no way I'm cooking for Liccle Bit. He doesn't appreciate good food. How could he ever tell me the Alabama Fried Chicken Hut on Crongton Broadway is better than mine?*

3:59 p.m.

I took the shortcut to school through Johnny Osbourne Lane.

Oh no! Road closed due to a police incident. Feds reeled out blue and white tape to block off the street. Peeps looking down from their tower block balconies. Sirens in the distance. I'm cursed.

I had to double back.

Went as fast as the scooter allowed, flying through the school gates at 4:13 p.m. I rolled to the Food Tech classroom and parked it on the end wall. Ms Penn couldn't believe it.

'I got it, Miss!' I wheezed. Every muscle in my body ached, I needed an oxygen bag and an IV drip – but I had the soft brown sugar!

Ten minutes later, Ms Penn let the audience in. They included the headmaster and the owner of the Cheesecake Lounge, Ms Aretha Berry. My friends Saira, Venetia, Liccle Bit, Jonah and Boy from the Hills bounced in too.

Everyone took their seats lining the walls of the classroom. I felt a buzz inside of me like I've never experienced it before.

4:39 p.m.

'Bakers!' Ms Penn called. 'Go!

I've baked this untold times before. It was one of the first desserts my mum taught me to bake. I closed my eyes and imagined the perfect rum, mango and apple crumble.

I took out a bowl and placed my flour into it. Added butter and mixed it in with my fingertips. Then I dropped in the soft brown sugar, porridge oats and crushed biscuits. I stirred like a mad DJ mixing hot tunes in a nightclub in Ibiza.

I took out a glass baking dish and dropped the mango chunks and apple pieces into it. I poured over a shot of Jamaican rum and the fruit juices and topped everything with my crumble mix.

I glanced at the audience.

Saira started a chant. 'McKay! McKay! McKay!'

I couldn't help but grin when I slapped my crumble into the oven. *Just got to wait till it turns golden brown.*

I wished Pops was here to see me. He'd be well proud. I already knew Mum was looking down on me.

Now it was just a waiting game.

Did I measure the quantities right? Did I tip in the right amount of

rum? Will the judges love it?

Finally, it was time. I served up my portions and waited for the judges to call me forward.

My dish was judged last. The headmaster, Ms Aretha Berry and Ms Penn sampled my crumble – they actually finished all of it! Ms Berry smiled. There were bits of crumble sticking to the corners of her mouth. The judges returned to their seats.

They spoke to each other in quiet voices and marked their scores on a sheet of paper.

Something was going in my stomach and my kidneys and intestines were having a mad fight.

The judging seemed to go on as long as double Chemistry.

Finally, Ms Penn stood up. My heart joined the war with my kidneys and intestines.

'All the dishes were of an incredibly high standard,' Ms Penn said. 'It was almost impossible to separate all the contestants. But there were two that were particularly outstanding.'

Suddenly, my knees felt unsteady. I thought I was gonna faint.

'In joint first place,' Ms Penn continued. 'Are Idolyn Cooper with her raspberry cheesecake . . . '

Please say my name, please say my name, please say my name.

'. . . And McKay Tambo with his rum, mango and apple crumble . . .'

On hearing my name, I leapt up into the air and let out a mighty roar. 'Yesssssss! Oh, my nights! Yesssssss!'

I slapped my palms on the counter to make a drumming sound and did a mad dance.

Ms Penn gave me one of her looks that told me to be quiet. 'They will share the fifty-pounds' worth of book tokens.'

The applause that rippled around the Food Tech classroom was even sweeter than my crumble.

Saira and Venetia hot-toed up and hugged me. Jonah and Boy from the Hills shook my hand. Liccle Bit stepped up to me – and even though he'd lost our bet he couldn't kill his grin. 'Congrats, bruv,' he said. 'Nuff respect times ten.'

'So, Bit,' I laughed. 'What is my best side? And I don't want no cheapo, second-hand portrait frame.'

Saira resumed her chant. 'McKay! McKay! McKay!'

I can't lie, I've never felt so good.

GOOD RECEPTION

SHARNA JACKSON
OLU OKE

Shernika!

So, what? You're too cute to answer texts now, is that it? I have to video call? You know this will nyam up my data, but it will be worth it. So—

Yeah, it will! There's no Wi-Fi on the bus, is there? This is Tottenham, remember? Not Tokyo.

Yep, I've good reception. Four full bars.

What do you mean, what have I done to my hair? You don't like it? Rude. That's how I had it yesterday, except the edges were laid and slick. Smooth smooth.

Of course, I put a headscarf on, Shernika, but what happens to it in the middle of the night is a mystery.

No, it's not allergic to my head. Or running away from my face – thanks for your theories, though. I'm doing my best to maintain it, innit? Mum hates putting heat on my hair, so this look is *rare*. I'm serving you a seasonal style, so you better appreciate it.

Yes, it *did* look better yesterday. So, are you going to let me tell you how it played out, or are you gonna keep chatting?

OK, so Saturday night, we—

Yes, I *know* Saturday wasn't yesterday – I know what day it is – let me give you context! So Saturday night, Leah—

My cousin? From Birmingham? Yeah! Her. I know – she's so cool! I miss her. Yeah, she came down and stayed at mine.

Nah, of course, we didn't sleep! Way too excited. Leah kept singing silly things in a jazzy way and we just kept creasing up. Proper cackling. Sides splitting. Eyes watering. At one point, right, it must have been like three in the morning, my Dad threw the bedroom door open, slamming it against the wall and shouted 'I don't want to hear another beep or a bop out of you!' into the darkness and that just made it worse.

It *was* funny. Guess you had to be there. So, next morning – I say next morning, it was like four hours later – we got up.

We were all right actually – too excited for tiredness.

No, we didn't eat then. After we washed, we drove over to Nanny Jean's. Our dresses were there, hanging up in Mum's old room, in those fancy garment bags. Like what businesswomen carry on planes? With the long zips? Yeah.

Yes, we ate there Shernika . . . why you always thinking about your gut? Like every meal's about to be a Last Supper or something?

That's not being rude to Jesus! I'm just saying . . .

Salmon and scrambled eggs on toasted muffins.

I know. Well it *was* a special occasion, that's why. Mum, Nanny Jean and Auntie Carol had this weird drink, too – fizzy wine mixed with orange juice.

No, I didn't try it. Ewww. No. Gross. Me and Leah had serious business to attend to anyhow.

So, then, me and Leah put on our dresses and stood in front of Nanny Jean's heavy red curtains for the photo I sent you. She said no shoes – she didn't want us tearing up her new carpet with our little heels. They hurt

a bit, anyway. Didn't you see the photo?

Too busy to look at a photo? Yeah, right. Let me resend. Got it?

Thanks! Yeah, the pattern bangs, right? Those little white lacy gloves were a step too far though, and when I tell you they were *itchy*. Lord. Leah threw hers away by lunchtime.

No, I'm not telling you about the meal yet.

I'll tell you about Auntie Carol, instead. She stepped down the stairs and she looked like an actual princess. Tiana time, for real. You know I'm not one for princesses or them fairytale things there, but she looked amazing in her long, silky dress and her headpiece, with the embroidered flowers. Nanny Jean couldn't take it. She was sniffing, weeping and dabbing at her eyes. Well cute. I'll send you a photo.

I know, right? *Stunning.*

His name is Paul, Shernika, and no – he wasn't there, was he? Don't you know anything about weddings? That's bad luck! If he saw her before the wedding, they'd be divorced in like six months or something.

Well, that's what Nanny Jean said and I choose to believe her. *She* knows stuff.

Hmmm . . . yeah, they *did* break up for a bit, a little while ago. Mum and Auntie Carol were whispering about it.

I don't know *exactly* what they said, but it wasn't a conversation for me and Leah. I could tell.

No. I'm not going to ask them now. So, where was I? Yeah. So, this fancy white car, white ribbon—

As *if* you know about cars.

Fine, fine. Rolls Royce, I think? I don't know. It came and got me, Leah and Auntie Carol. The three of us sat in the back, Leah and I squeezed up next to her but doing our very best to not crease her dress. Auntie Carol sat in the middle, and we sat on either side of her, each holding a hand, our bouquet of flowers on our laps.

Nah, she didn't want to run away! At least, I don't think she did. She was quiet though, and stared out of the window for a lot of the drive.

I guess she was nervous. I would be. Wouldn't you?

Yeah, well I thought I was never getting married either, but after being at this wedding, I might just change my mind.

I don't know to who!

The ceremony was nice, yeah! Me and Leah walked in first, and then I got why Auntie Carol was nervous. All eyes were on us. I had to walk in a strange way, in time with Leah. When I looked over her, she started whisper singing in that jazzy voice again, which made me snort. I had to look down at my shoes to make sure I didn't get in trouble with my mum and dad. If I embarrassed them in front of all of those people, phew, well, I wouldn't be on the phone with you now. It would be over for me.

We sat down, Auntie Carol came in and everyone gasped. Paul was crying hard in his green suit. It was well sweet.

Yeah, awww is right!

No, I don't think they were guilty tears, Shernika.

The rest of the ceremony was a lot of talking and singing, but it was nice, yeah. The kissing bit was a little cringe. I had to look away.

Ewww, Shernika, stop! That's disgusting.

Well, we went to take photographs in the churchyard. The man behind the camera was well extra, whooping and hollering to everyone smiling at the same time. Like a jester.

I *know* it's his job – I respect that – but he was annoying. And my feet were starting to hurt. Way too much standing around on gravel and grass in those pinching shoes.

So, then we went to the reception – it was the *best* bit. It was a *great* reception.

Shernika . . . it was *fancy*. Cheese soufflé to start. Slow-cooked beef with buttermilk creamed potatoes for mains and a flourless chocolate cake for dessert.

Yes, I know you love chocolate cake—

Curry goat and rice when the less important guests came in the evening. Yes, we have a fridge full of leftovers. Yes, you can have some.

There were speeches, mostly unfunny in truth, but Auntie Carol and Paul got Leah and me matching bracelets so we'd remember this day forever – like we'd forget!

At this point, my feet were on fire, my hair was starting to come loose, and, secretly, I was up for changing out of my dress and into some shorts, but I didn't care. I threw my shoes towards Mum and ran back to the floor. When I tell you I danced, Shernika, I *danced*. Remember me at the Year Five school disco? When I was unstoppable? Times that by ten.

Yeah. I didn't know I had it in me, either. But right there and then, seeing Auntie Carol and Paul being so in love, my stomach full of fine food, feeling the bass of brilliant music in my

bones, just did . . . *something* to me. Right then, swaying on the floor, my arms wrapped around Leah's neck, everyone dressed so nicely, everybody in great moods, I wished I could live there, in that moment forever. Or if not, bottle all that energy, all those incredibly good vibes and carry it with me, in my pocket, for all time. And just open it, whenever I needed a boost. I'd sell it, and become a millionaire overnight.

I know, if only that was possible, right? Anyway, Shernika, next stop is mine, and no one's rung the bell yet. I'm gonna have to walk down the stairs when the bus is moving and you know how much I love that.

Ha! Of course. You wouldn't have liked it – it was full of currants and dried fruit and had thick icing. I know, you'd have chocolate cake. Of course, you would.

WHO SAID SUMMER WAS FUN?

YASMIN JOSEPH
DENZELL DANKWAH

Everyone says that summer is fun, but I was still waiting.

Six whole weeks of tracing the block with my fingers like a maze . . . boring.

Dad says the fun is outside and I won't know until I go out and find it. He opens the curtains before he leaves for work and lets the sun's rays beam into my chest until I'm charged awake like a battery.

'Vitamin D, son. Look lively. Early bird catches the worm.'

Well I don't like birds, a pigeon once stole the sandwich from my meal deal and worms are even worse, so where's the fun in that? He just chuckles while I squeeze my eyes shut.

Mum says that the fun is inside.

'There's only trouble out there. Fun is with your family.' She says this as she twitches our curtains, shaking her head and sighing about how 'this one' was once such a good child, and how she needs to catch up with 'that one's' mother when she next sees her around.

Mum says fun is in the first crispy bite of the fried dumplings she makes whilst singing to Beres when she's in a good mood.

She says it's in watching the flowers bloom that we planted together on the balcony. How the greens and reds clash against the bricks, protecting us in a rainforest of our own making. She says fun is in spending quality time with my big sister Cara and – I stop her there. That is definitely not fun.

∗ ∗ ∗

The other day Marcus from 39A came round uninvited. He's been doing this pretty much every day since we first learned to walk three weeks apart.

He sat at the end of my bed, chewing loudly and blowing huge bubbles with his gum. He picked up a controller and started pressing and fiddling. Interrupting my game without asking to add a second player, just mashing up my top score.

My spacecraft went tumbling into a black hole. I jumped up.

'Relaaax!' he said, smiling, his voice always deep and droopy like butter. But I told him he had no idea. I had ten seconds to save the planet! I was so close. The hard work. The many calculated missions. The new discoveries of life I would've made in the next level.

He just leaned back and smiled.

'You've gotta chill, Jojo man. It's just a game, there's always tomorrow.

We're having fun.' Then he ate one of my biscuits. That was the final straw.

'What do you know about fun, Marcus?' He looked at me like my question made no sense. Like he was the Master of Fun. King Fun himself.

'Pffft. No point even telling you. Not like you'd even get it.'

'Try me.' I said.

'I know lots about fun. I have fun all the time.'

'Really? Doing what?'

'. . . Stuff.'

'Stuff like what?'

Marcus took a few seconds to think. 'You're gonna laugh.'

'I won't.'

'You will.'

'Just say.'

'. . . Dancing.'

I squashed my mouth up into a ball. I've known Marcus my whole life and I've never seen him dance. I can't even imagine his long arms and legs making those shapes. The most movement I've ever seen this boy do is to and from my fridge, or maybe lifting his eyebrows.

'Dancing?' I said, unsure. He nodded.

'I just like how it feels. You know when people throw their hands up in the air begging for more music, and everyone's dripping with sweat and happiness, and the bass is just rattling through the soles of your trainers and making your knees shake like this?' He demonstrated and I burst out laughing. We both did.

'Marcus, you ain't never been to no place like that. Your curfew's five o'clock.'

'Yeah I have. My brother took me. You don't believe me?'

'Sure. Just like your dad got a Lamborghini but exchanged it for a van with more leg room.'

'He did, you could ask him. He just don't like talking about it.'

'You ain't ever been to no place like that.'

'I have . . . and I'd take you with me if you'd leave the house.'

Sometimes when Marcus says things I don't like, I try not to react. Because he has a way of making my skin feel like it's made of glass. Like we're so used to being beside each other, that he can see right into my head and I can't have any secrets.

I took one of my biscuits and sank back into the chair.

✳ ✳ ✳

Yesterday there was a heatwave and it felt like my wallpaper could've dripped off and slid down into to the flat below. When Mum got back from shopping she slipped her head around my door and said, 'If you put it away quick enough you'll see a surprise at the bottom.' Smiling and looking happy with herself.

'Two seconds, Mum . . . just two more seconds . . .' And as I steered the spacecraft, racing through the galaxy I felt cool air blowing on my skin. Earth shrank further and further behind me as the stars twisted into shapes which gave me clues about my future. I felt tiny in the universe and the great darkness of the sky wrapped around my shoulders tightly like a blanket or a hug. I was doing something that had never been done before. A new level. I was a hero.

My body was light as a feather, my snacks floated around me, no time to pin them down. Streams of bright light were trailing behind. I wondered who was watching. Seconds away from making history. From safety. From the great unknown when—

Blackout.

Mum stood in front of me with the remote. 'Jojo? I asked you to put the shopping away an hour ago!'

She searched around the console looking for the eject button. Took my game and at the door quietly said, 'That's enough now. It's your summer holiday and the world will be much better with you in it. Can't be losing you in space.'

When Mum's worried she does this thing with her hands, twists them together like she's draining water from a cloth. She stared at me like we were miles apart. Why can't I just stay in here and do what I want? I'm not hurting anyone. Why does everyone tiptoe in this room like the floor is made of lava?

✳ ✳ ✳

In the kitchen at the bottom of the shopping bag I found Mum's surprise. Vanilla ice cream, my favourite. The tub had tipped on its side and the ice cream had completely melted so it was leaking through the cracks. Gooey paste stuck to everything. Yuck. I wiped it off as I stacked the things away.

Noises and colours floated from the living room with the six o'clock news. Drums, helicopters, reds and blues, voices shouting – some of them sounded like ours. Every day on the television there were reasons for people to be hurt and angry. To come together in the streets creating a sea of faces and signs. Mum asked to change to her decorating show.

'This news is too miserable,' she said. Dad sighed.

'The world won't stop spinning if we choose to stop looking. It'll only make us more dizzy.'

Cara talked over the TV with her best friend on the phone, convinced they could do a better job of reporting. I wondered if the news was this noisy in everyone else's homes. If it boomed through the walls like dropping pots and pans. My fingers were sticky with ice cream, glued to everything I touched. My game was gone.

Who said summer was fun?

The doorbell rang. Marcus.

As I opened up the blue sky poured over his shoulders. A bit of air came in, and for a second the entire house and all of its walls took a deep breath. I could hear laughter from a football game going on in the square below.

'You coming out?'

'Where you going?'

'Nowhere really . . . shop. Mum needs avocados for dinner. Was gonna say we should take our bikes.'

'Can't.'

'Let me guess. A special space mission . . .'

'Nah. Just made a mess. Gotta tidy up.' Marcus looked over my shoulder.

'Don't look too bad.'

When we were finished Mum came in the kitchen to inspect the job. Cara tried to say that we'd missed a spot but Mum just laughed and said we could go.

* * *

We raced to the end of our road. Mum called over the balcony. 'Careful boys!' Our feet spun in loops trying to push our bikes as fast as they could go.

'I'm gonna win!' Marcus huffed.

'You wish,' I wheezed.

'My mum says the change is mine. Winner gets to keep it.'

We picked up the pace. At the finish line I imagined the streets filling with cheers. Cameras. People bursting out from the post office, the chip shop, anywhere they could to catch a glimpse of our speed. And as me and Marcus screeched to a halt we fell into an untidy pile under our bikes, laughing.

'A draw,' he said after a moment's thought. I was happy with that.

Marcus's mum said to make sure that the avocados were ripe, so we squeezed ten of them in a row to check. Then Marcus started to juggle the two he thought were best. I tried to copy him and dropped mine on the floor. The shopkeeper said we had to pay for them all.

The change was enough for one vanilla ice cream so we sat by our bikes with two wooden spoons waiting for the fire in our legs to cool down. Marcus played some music on his phone and then he started showing me this funny dance move. It looked looked like electricity was travelling through his pointed fingers to his neck and spine.

The sun baked the pavement and the gravel in the road began to sparkle like glitter. A bright red convertible zoomed by. We leant forward to watch it go until there was nothing but a dot in the distance and then we took turns guessing where it was going.

We talked about our futures. Marcus was going to be a doctor and a music producer. I was going to be an engineer or somebody who studied plant life – we were both still going to be neighbours. Our dreams sat above our heads and sometimes met in the middle.

The blue of the sky began to wash into orange and yellow and we knew it was time to head home. We took the long route back by the canal because Marcus heard there'd been sightings of snakes round there. I wasn't convinced.

But something in my world had changed. It was like the same streams of light surrounding the spacecraft in my game were quietly trailing behind our bikes. The miracles waiting in the stars above us zoomed down towards our block. The bags of bruised avocados attached to our handles floated without gravity and we were full of laughs and stories, mixed with ice cream but somehow still weightless, safe.

Marcus noticed the smile on my face.

'You having fun?'

My Body Knows Beats

ZAÏRE KRIEGER

ASHLEY EVANS

My limbs know
how the drimming of the drums go
shamelessly moving
closing my eyes
my figure and sound in an endless chase
no matter what happens,
I will always have this space

these steps
they're not just steps,
they are the markings of feet from ages ago
when no clocks tick-tock'ed
when no media for moves bartered
no matter who comes and goes,
I will always have a partner

In my mind
I'm on a stage in front of millions of strangers' eyes
but the beat to me familiar
we can get away, together
travelling far and wide
no matter how old I grow,
I will always stay this child

LOST AND FOUND

KELECHI OKAFOR
DORCAS MAGBADELO

You are going to the shop to buy seasoning cubes for mum.

When I say 'you', well, I am you and you are me, only you're ten years old and I'm much older now. I see you but you can't see me because to you, I don't exist yet. You can't think past being ten years old. OK, maybe you can think past it a little bit, since you keep asking Mum if you can get those cool black shoes with a little bit of a chunky heel when you start high school.

'Kelechi . . . Kelechiiiiiiii!' Mum is shouting from the kitchen. You walk in and she's holding onto her purse in one hand, and our baby brother in the other.

'Yes Mummy,' you say. I look at Mum through my mind's eye and how young she looks with the light gleaming through the window that leads to the garden – making her eyes shimmer.

'Here is the money for the seasoning cubes. Be careful when you are walking to Peckham because you know there are gbomo gbomo everywhere.'

'I'll be careful and not talk to strangers and run really fast if anybody tries to talk to me.' Mum seems pleased with this response. Even at the age of thirty-five, Mum still reminds me to be careful of kidnappers. She is hilarious sometimes.

Mum holds out a fifty pound note.

You are in shock. That is a lot of money!

Mum is looking at you impatiently.

'Will you take the money or do you want to stand here like a statue forever?'

You take the fifty pound note and inspect it. All because Mum doesn't have any change, you have been given the massive responsibility of going to Peckham and back with this smooth, crispy, brightly-coloured money.

You feel grown-up.

Trainers on. Thick black coat in hand even though it is summer and very hot outside. You wear this coat whenever you are outside. It makes you

feel safe because sometimes you get nervous being around other people.

As you reach for the door, Mum chides from the kitchen bathed in light,

'Kelechi, that fifty pound note is a lot of money. So be careful! If you lose the money, you had better just lose yourself with it.'

Even though you have heard Mum say this before, it still makes you stand up super straight with fear. You are going to be extremely careful on the way to the shop.

You walk by the playground next to the community hall. You pass by the block of flats, then the houses that form a big square just as you emerge onto Peckham High Street. You have been in London for five years since moving over from Lagos, Nigeria to live with Mum, yet sometimes when you walk through Peckham it is like some of Lagos came along with you to make sure you would be okay. The shop you are headed to is one that stocks mainly Nigerian groceries. It's things like these that help us to not feel so homesick.

It is so hot outside. You still don't want to take the big black coat off. This is the part where I wish I could tell you that one day you will ditch the coat because you will begin to understand that you are brilliant and unique and you do not need to shy away from being noticed.

Reggae music blares out of a car driving past. Laughter cascades through the air from a group of kids a bit older than you as they lounge on their bicycles. The boys with their cool trainers and the girls with lollipops adorning their slicked-up hairstyles. They all look so cool and happy. The sweet aroma of suya grilling in a shack in front of a car wash wafts through the SE15 air.

You are outside the shop now and you check your pocket for the money before you step inside. Oh no.

The fifty pound note isn't there.

It isn't in the right pocket or the left. Your tummy seizes up immediately from fear. Sweat beads start forming on your forehead from the heat of your big black coat and from the anticipation of how much trouble you are going to be in when you get home and tell Mum that you lost the money.

Panic is slowly setting in, disappointment too. With two much younger brothers at times it feels like you are not noticed. It isn't a good idea to get noticed by Mum for losing money.

'Money doesn't grow on trees you know!' She is always reminding you. The old woman who owns the Nigerian shop looks over at you quizzically hanging around in the doorway, right by the basket overflowing with fresh plantain. Before she can ask you what is the matter, you shut the door to retrace your steps.

You are walking back home but it's like you are wading through mud. Your legs don't want to move. Way too scared of having to explain how in heavens you managed to lose the money for seasoning cubes.

You pass by the same car that was playing reggae music as it drove by earlier. It is parked up now and the music is still blaring. What a tune! You can't enjoy it though because you start considering whether you might have to move out of the flat because you lost the money. Could Mum have been serious about that?

As you walk slowly past the group of older kids still laughing, suddenly their laughter is annoying. You envy that they can be so carefree. Probably because they haven't just lost a large amount of money.

Your flat is in view now. Oh no. Out of desperation you do something that you only do when you are in serious need of comfort and help even at ten years old.

You pray.

You walk and say your prayer quietly because you know that God hears our hearts and not just our words so you could pray in a whisper if you really wanted to.

'Dear God, sometimes I think I've lost you because bad things happen. But other times I find you again and I feel safe. I need your help. I've lost Mum's fifty pound note and I'm scared that I will be in a lot of trouble if I don't find it. I know the money is probably long gone by now but if it's not and you help me find it, I will do something nice for you. I mean you're God and you have everything but I've gotten really good at making friendship bracelets . . .'

You are rambling now. I can tell you that years later, I still pray in the same way. You stand still for a few minutes waiting for a response.

Nothing. OK. You sigh. Time to face Mum. You walk past the playground next to the community hall when a light wind blows by and something moving to your right catches your eye. What is that?

Oh. My. God.

Wrapped in-between one of the railings by the playground is the fifty pound note. You quickly grab the money and squeal with joy. How is that even possible? By every probability the money should've been long gone. Your legs feel light again. Your tummy starts to unknot. You are still sweating though. No longer from panic, but because you are still shrouded in the big black coat. You feel so elated and so, so thankful. You thank God for getting back to you so quickly.

It must seem like you've been gone for ages. So you race back to the shops. You are really good at running fast. Whizzing by the hustle and bustle of Peckham. You grab the seasoning cubes from the middle shelf, not

too far from the bags of Ijebu and Igbo Garri. You thank the old lady who owns the shop as you pay, 'thank you Auntie,' because even in a rush you still have to remember to call your Nigerian elders auntie and uncle even when you are not related! She smiles at you with the same quizzical look from earlier, then mutters, 'You children of nowadays, so much energy!'

You get home and Mum is on the phone to one of her friends as your baby brother sleeps in his cot and your three year old brother draws on the wallpaper (Mum will notice soon enough and scream. Haha).

'Here you go, Mum!'

'That was quick! Well done. Pop it in the kitchen along with the change.'

Quick? Quick? You feel like you have been gone for a lifetime. Time flies when you're not losing money you guess.

What an adventure. You slump on the bed and now in my mind's eye I am looking at your beaming, joyful face thinking about all that you have

just been through.

I don't believe time to be linear. Which is why I reach for you in this moment of joy and we become an 'us'. We will continue to experience moments like these all throughout our life.

By that I mean that we will experience losing things, we will lose people, and even feel like we have lost ourselves sometimes. But as we get older, we will realize that any time we feel that we've lost something, an opportunity for joy is created when we either retrace our steps back to those things and people, or we discover alternative things that fit into our life in a more beautiful way.

I trace my steps into my memory world and find the timeline where a moment like losing and finding the fifty pound note serves as a reminder that there are precious pockets in time when we have experienced miracles.

I wish you knew – ten year old me – that you are very brave, even when you don't feel like it. People now tell me how fearless and confident they believe me to be and most of them don't know about you and our big black coat.

Without you there wouldn't be a me and there would be no us, so thank you for praying and believing you would be heard. The joy I experience now can only be because of your belief.

Sunshine Girl

CAMRYN GARRETT

CHARIS JB

The library was the best place in the whole wide world.

Of course, it wasn't a palace. It smelt like mildew. There weren't any TVs, or video games. And there were hardly any people there most of the time. But that was the best part. The lack of people was what made the school library my palace.

Bear Valley Middle School had way too many people squished into the same tiny space. Whenever I walked through the halls, it felt like I was being crushed. My entire middle school experience felt like trying to breathe underwater. Unable to break the surface and catch a breath.

The library made things a little bit easier. It was an escape.

'Seventh grade isn't forever,' Ms Anderson, the librarian, would say as she led me through to the animal section. 'As long as you can get through the rest of the year, you'll be fine. Pretty soon you'll be off to high school.'

Just the thought of it made me shudder. If middle school was drowning in the pool, high school would be like drowning in the ocean without a life jacket, or one of those red things lifeguards tossed around to save people.

My only friends were my bunnies. I'd found them while walking to school one early spring day, nestled in the bushes behind the elementary school's playground. I couldn't find their mama, and they looked so alone, all piled up on each other with their eyes closed.

I'd hurried to the school library, asking Ms Anderson to give me every single book she had on rabbits.

Now their home was a gigantic cardboard box that I'd borrowed from my daddy's store. I kept it nestled between some bushes near the gate at the back of the school. No one ever comes back there. Not even the janitors.

'Hey, Peaches,' I cooed as I hurried back there, dropping my backpack beside them. There were five little bunnies in total. Even though the big box seemed like it had more than enough room for all of them, there was no telling when they'd get big enough to go out into the world. But the thought of the bunnies, all alone, with no one to take care of them, killed me.

In the meantime, I fussed over them as much as I could. I made sure that their home was nestled in the shade, and that a window screen with holes punched through rested on top of the box so that they wouldn't jump out. According to the books Ms Anderson gave me, they needed to be fed twice a day: once at dusk, and once at dawn.

I nestled into my favourite spot, snuggling Peaches in my arms.

I had to organize Mr Smith's shelves to get free milk and supplies, but it was worth it. The bunnies were old enough now to drink the formula from a little dish that I left in their home, but I missed the way that their tiny whiskers used to twitch when I fed them myself.

I leaned against the fence, and watched as the bunnies hurried to eat. There was Speckles, who had big patches of white on his dark fur.

Then there was Peaches, whose fur was a light red colour. Cookie and Brownie got their names because I was pretty hungry when I found them.

And last was Ducky, who always looked like he was smiling when I came near.

After feeding, I usually watched them hop around in the grass for a while. I didn't mind them wandering – as long as they didn't go too far. I'd just have to be back home before Mom. She was working late shifts at the hospital tonight, and Daddy would be at the grocery store. Both too busy to notice that I was out every evening.

'Are those your bunnies?'

I jumped. No one ever came back here, especially not at dusk. Nobody.

My eyes froze on the girl. It was rare to see someone with brown skin at Bear Valley Middle School. Even rarer to see someone who looked like this girl, with skin so dark that it reflected the sun.

The girl blinked her dark eyes at me. Like she expected me to answer her.

Technically, no, they weren't my bunnies. I knew they wouldn't be able to stay with me forever. But they were my friends.

Only, I didn't exactly want to tell the girl that. I didn't need her running back into school the next day, telling everyone I was a weirdo who could only make friends with animals.

She just smiled, a dimple showing in her left cheek.

'It's okay,' she whispered. 'I won't tell.'

And she pressed a finger to her lips, just to prove it.

* * *

One of the other worst parts of Bear Valley Middle School was that no one looked like me. Being here made me feel like I was the only person with dark skin and dark eyes and lumpy braids in my head to match.

It felt weird talking about it, too. Back at Jackson, my old school, my teachers talked a lot about race. We had Diversity Day, where Carlos Vasquez brought his abuela's empanadas, Black History Month assemblies, and classes where you just talked about what it was like to be not-white in America. But not at Bear Valley. There were a few other brown kids, but they weren't in my advanced Science and Math classes. I knew I wasn't the only smart one, but the teachers at Bear Valley didn't seem to see anything weird about seeing only white faces in the top classes. Everyone acted like it was just the way things were. It was even unusual to see anyone who looked like me in the library.

Until today, anyway.

'Class, remember that we're here to do research,' the plump teacher declared as she led her class into my safe haven. 'I don't want to see any fooling around on the computers, or any other horseplay. Is that understood?'

That's when I saw her. She looked like she was laughing at something the girl next to her said. Her head was tilted back, just right, so that the sunlight from the window hit her face. It was like the sun couldn't help but find her.

She turned, and my eyes darted back down.

When I glanced back up, the girl was still staring. There was even a smile on her face, dimple and all. She waved, like we were old friends.

I cracked my book back open, wishing that I could disappear into my seat. Hoping that the weird tingling in my stomach would disappear along with me.

✻ ✻ ✻

I'd only had a crush on one person before. His name was Carlos, the same boy who'd brought empanadas and tres leches and homemade hot chocolate to school on a rotating schedule every Diversity Day. His skin was tan, like warm caramel, and his smile was always bright.

I hadn't felt that way since.

I thought about it later, while trudging back to give the bunnies their dusk feeding. Maybe I did have a crush. A crush like the girls in class whispered and passed notes about. Only it wasn't like that at all. It wasn't like I was ever going to tell her.

I sighed, bending down beside the box. 'Hey, guys. I hope you've had a better day than me. I mean—'

The words died down when I realized that they weren't listening. After all, they couldn't listen if they weren't in the box.

'Guys?' I called out, like they would actually answer. 'Cookie? Brownie? Peaches?'

I dropped to my knees, digging my fingers into the fence. They couldn't have made it under there, there wasn't enough room. They were getting too big.

'Speckles?' I called out hopefully, turning around. Where could they have gone? Their legs were so little. They wouldn't have been able to make it that far.

'Ducky?' My voice cracked, just a little bit, as I swung my backpack full of supplies over my shoulder. They couldn't have gone far. Maybe I could still find them before it got dark.

'Are those their names? I like them.'

I knew who it was before I turned around. Her sneakers were smeared with mud, and her shirt was damp with sweat. Maybe she was one of those sporty girls, who tried to force their way onto every team the school had.

'What are you even doing here?' I snapped, running a hand through my braids.

She stepped back, startled, like I had pushed her.

'Why didn't you wave at me in the library?' She asked, cocking her head to the side. Instead of multiple braids like me, she just had one.

I swallowed. She'd noticed that?

'I didn't notice,' I lied, shifting from foot to foot. 'I was reading.'

She bit her lip, looking a whole lot like she didn't believe me. 'What's your name?'

'Nora.'

'Mine's Sadie.'

Sadie.

'Great.'

'Why are you calling your bunnies?'

I sighed, swallowing back tears. 'I think they're lost.'

'Oh. Wow.' Her eyes widened. 'That's not good.'

I rolled my eyes, tugging at my backpack strap. I could've told her that.

'Yeah. Well, I have to go look for them before dark.' I shrugged. 'Sorry about ignoring you in the library.'

'You said you didn't notice me,' she fired back, eyes narrowed. 'Liar.'

My face burned. Nice move, Nora.

'I can help you find them,' she said, filling the silence. 'They couldn't have gone far, right? They looked so little yesterday.'

This could take a million times longer with her trailing behind me the entire time.

But she was still smiling and she liked their names and she offered, so it'd be pretty rude not to let her come along.

'Yeah,' I said, gesturing for her to follow me. 'You can help.'

She grinned, and I felt part of myself melting.

✲ ✲ ✲

One thing I learned about Sadie fairly quickly: she asked questions. A lot of them.

'Why don't you ever come outside during lunch?'

'I eat in the library.'

'Why don't you talk outside of class?'

'I don't know what I'm supposed to say.'

'Why did you switch schools?'

'The Science programme. The library.'

'So you wanna be a scientist when you grow up?'

'A veterinarian, actually.'

As we walked, I narrowed my eyes at the ground, hoping to see a flash of red or white. We needed to hurry. There were all sorts of animals that came out at night, animals that wouldn't hesitate to eat little bunnies.

I started walking a little faster. Sadie hurried behind me.

'Do you have a boyfriend?'

I stumbled over my feet a little. 'What?'

Sadie blinked at me, like it was a perfectly normal question.

'Do. You. Have. A—'

'No,' I started, shaking my head. 'Uh, I don't.'

'I don't either.'

I'm not sure what she expected me to do with that information. My stomach squirmed a little bit, letting me know that it had an idea.

'You know,' Sadie started, voice cautious. I could feel her eyes on me, even though I focused on the ground. 'These were wild rabbits that you found out in the grass, right?'

'Without their mom. Yeah.'

'Maybe they left because it was time. I mean, I don't think that wild bunnies are supposed to be pets.' She paused. 'If you want a pet bunny, I'm sure you can go to the pet store and—'

'That's not what this is about,' I snapped. She didn't know what it was like to not have any friends. She sure seemed to have them in the library. And she definitely didn't get what it was like being friends with bunnies. Always worrying about their safety. Wondering if they were eating correctly. Reading thousands of books just to figure out how to take care of them.

'I'm just trying to help.' Sadie paused, eyes wide. 'You don't have to get mad.'

'Let's just stop talking,' I mumbled, hurrying along. 'We're never going to find them if we keep wasting time.'

Sadie was silent, even though I heard her footsteps behind me.

* * *

When we stopped at the big tree for a break, the sun was just starting to set. That meant that Mom was home. That meant that Daddy was just starting to close up the store.

'You know, I didn't mean to make you mad,' Sadie started, cutting through the silence. 'I was just trying to help.'

I stared down at my fingers. I didn't have the guts to tell her that I knew.

'I'm sorry,' I mumbled instead.

'Why are you so upset about the bunnies, anyway?'

I sucked in a deep breath.

'Well, for one thing, they might not be able to eat the grass that's around them. Bigger animals might eat them. They won't have milk. They could get cold, or scared, or—'

'OK,' Sadie interrupted, wide eyed, but I kept going.

'And they're my friends, and you can't just let your friends get hurt.'

Once the words were out of my mouth, I knew it was over. Sadie was going to start laughing in my face. She'd pull out her phone and start texting her friends about how lame I was.

But I was surprised to feel her hand slipping into mine.

'I'll be your friend,' she said. Her voice was soft, but seemed to echo in my ears. 'And I'll make sure that you don't get hurt, OK?'

Instead of answering, I glanced down at our hands. And I squeezed back.

* * *

It wasn't night-time when we started walking back, but it sure was something close. The sky was a dark blue, but the reds and oranges and yellows were still there. There weren't going down without a fight.

Sadie and I were still holding hands. When she pulled away, I glanced over in confusion.

'What is it?' I asked.

She pointed a finger toward a patch of grass.

I swallowed.

The bunnies – my bunnies – were all gathered around a bigger bunny. Their mama. Tears stung at my eyes as I realized this might be the last time I'd see them. Sure, I'd miss heading over to see them every day, but this was their mom. Their family.

'I told you that they'd be okay.' Sadie turned to me with a huge smile.

There was that stupid tugging in my stomach again, so I did it. I leaned forward to press my lips against hers, to try to catch her by surprise like the guys did in the movies, but she turned. I hit her cheek instead.

I stared in shock, my cheeks flaming. Stupid Nora.

'I'm sorry!' Her laugh bubbled through the air. 'I didn't know that's what you were trying to do.'

'Wait, you aren't mad?' I blinked at her. 'I tried to kiss you.'

'Why would I be mad?' She cocked her head. 'Don't you kiss people you like?'

I probably should've said something smooth, the way Daddy did when Mom was mad at him, but nothing would come out. I was too distracted.

She liked me.

Sadie pressed a softer kiss to my cheek.

'You worry too much, Nora,' she said, a giggle in her voice.

As we watched the bunnies happily hop away together, I realized that I didn't feel sad. I wasn't alone any more. Now I had Sadie, who made me feel warm and special and a little like magic. I felt happy, like it was Christmas morning.

She smiled, lacing her hand in mine. She gave it a squeeze.

I squeezed harder.

STICKS AND STONES

KOLEKA PUTUMA
SNALO NGCABA

An ode to the imagination weavers
spinning bambaram on street corners,
trading monopoly for marbles,

who ride with the top down
in convertibles made with wire and bottle caps for tires,
going around the block for all to see,
dressed in their Sunday best on Christmas and New Years Eve,

who spy with their little eyes
when they hide 'n' seek,

who seek refuge
in long traditions of Unopey'ntana,
tying every black girl who has gathered for
Diketo / Upuca / Magava / Ukugenda,
and bargained in
Morabaraba / Ncuva / Morula;

stones fit for more than building,
they carve lineages on dirt roads,
around potholes, on varnished verandas,
down the street, inside and next to spaza shops:

bompies drip down chins,
hands, oily and sticky from lollipops and amagwinya,
hold worlds only their imagination can orchestrate.

hopscotch lifts bodies
up to the sky,

made-up language winds around
hips and legs swinging,
tickled and threatened by Kgati / Ntimo /
Ugqaphu.

every body has a turn,
every body keeps score:
Three Tins, Moruba, Fushu,
Banyana ke di bom bom, Hambo thengi
OMO, Isikipa sika Jomo,
on on

on and on

until the street lights
call them home,

until the street lights
called us home.

Halloween Dance

FUNMBI OMOTAYO
MICHAEL KENNEDY

It's close to midnight and something evil is lurking in the dark.

Actually it's closer to eight o'clock on the morning of 31 October. Halloween. And there's no actual evil lurking, especially after the morning prayer session me and my family just had. I'm pretty sure my parents cast out every last evil spirit in East London.

No, it's just me, Tobi Adenuga, practising my dance moves to 'Thriller'. Today is a big day for me. Just last week my school announced the annual Halloween party and it's been the talk of the school ever since.

Halloween parties are always lit. The teachers transform the school to look like a haunted house, we all get to dress up and the kid with the best costume wins a prize. But this year I had my sights set on something bigger.

Best Dancer.

I had signed up for the dance competition and there was a lot riding on it, especially after last year's disaster. A failed attempt at the splits caused my Green Goblin costume to tear right down the middle exposing my Superman underwear for the whole world to see. The entire school burst out laughing: even some of the teachers were holding back giggles. My humiliation was complete when certified school bully Warren Bailey yelled out, 'Look everyone, it's Superpants!'

That memory still haunts me now. I should have known better than to risk the splits. When my mum said she would pick up a Green Goblin costume for me, I was imagining a branded outfit from a fancy dress place or at least an elaborate homemade version. But what I got was a three-pack of lime green leotards from the local pound store.

'You can even use it for your pyjamas!' Mum said when she saw the expression on my face, as if that was some sort of consolation.

Obviously, this year's costume had to be flawless. After days of deliberation I had decided to go as Dracula, slick and smooth with an air of danger. And a smart dresser – no leotards in sight. It was perfect. I enlisted the help of my older sister, Tola, who was more than happy to oblige. She was present at last year's Superpants disaster and had to bear some of the shame, so she wasn't about to let me embarrass the family name two years in a row. She was part of a street dance team so I trusted her judgement (and her ability to improve my moves).

The only problem: convincing my God-fearing parents to pay for a costume to help me dress up like a monster who drinks blood like it's strawberry Ribena. It would be close to impossible. I'd have to get creative.

Coming from a church background did have its advantages – my church clothes of black shoes, trousers and a plain white shirt made for a perfect Dracula outfit. Tola lent me this burgundy waistcoat with a swirl leaf pattern and matching bow-tie which added to the look. The cape was the tricky part – the closest thing in the house was my father's agbada, a free-flowing robe with wide sleeves worn by men in West Africa – great for wedding ceremonies but not ideal for Halloween.

Luckily my parents had allowed me to wash dishes in their restaurant

for a fee of ten pounds. It was enough for me to buy my very own cape, a black knee-length number with a collar and silky red lace interior. I won't lie, it looked crazy fam! I even managed to get my hands on some vampire fangs from a magazine that was giving them away. Finally, dressed and doing my best vampire pose in front of the mirror with the music on full blast, I must say I looked the part.

'Tobi! It's too early for this kind of noise. Ah, ah, what's going on here?' Mum burst into my room with a menacing look on her face as I rushed to turn down the music.

'Sorry Mum, I didn't see you there!'

'I've been calling you for the past one hour, what if I was dying?'

My parents love to exaggerate. We had only just finished praying ten minutes ago, so how could she have been calling me for the past hour?

'Is this how you are going to school?' she said, looking me up and down.

'No Mum, it's my Halloween costume for the school party later.'

'So you are going as the Devil?'

'Um, no. I'm going as Dracula.'

I could see the look on my mum's face change from menace to utter dismay.

'And who is Dracula please?' There was no good answer, so I just told her the truth.

'He's a vampire.' And with that, all hell broke loose.

'A vampire? LANRE!

Come and see your son, he wants to go to school dressed as a vampire!'
This was standard Nigerian parenting, call in the spouse for back-up, the ol' good cop/bad cop routine (except in most Nigerian homes, it was bad cop/bad cop).

'Ah, ah, you are looking sharp!'
My father was way more relaxed than my mum. He liked to think of himself as a cool dad.

'Lanre, don't encourage him please. You want him to go to school looking like Satan?'

'I'm not going to school like this, Mum, and I'm a vampire. Not Satan.'

'I don't care, they are both evil.'

'Tolu, leave him, it's just a Halloween costume. All the other kids will be dressed the same. Young man, go into my room and find some cufflinks. My son must stand out.'

I knew my dad would come through. I had to contain my excitement though as Mum was not impressed.

'Anyway, just don't be late for school,' she said as she stormed out of the room.

'Don't mind your mother, you know they didn't have parties in her day.

But she's right, don't be late for school.'

✽ ✽ ✽

Class seemed to go on forever. At lunch I went over to the hall to check out the decorations but all the windows were blacked out.

'Hey Tobi, what are you looking at?' It was Amanda Safo, the coolest girl in the whole school. She was also captain of the football team and had a mean right foot. I had the biggest crush on her but couldn't say anything – all the more reason for me to shine at this dance.

'Hey Amanda! I'm just trying to see what the school has in store for us this year. They're keeping a tight lid on this one. You're part of the planning committee, right?'

'Yes, but I missed the last few days. You know my sickle cell gets worse in cold weather.'

'Oh yeah, it's the same with me and my hay fever.'

'You get hay fever in cold weather?'

'Yeah, you know, it's an . . . autumnal . . . variant of hay fever. Very rare case.' Autumnal variant? Really Tobi? I knew I should cut my losses and leave before I said anything more absurd.

'Oh right,' she said laughing to herself. 'So who are you coming as this year? I really hope it involves tights.'

'I'm coming as Dracula actually, and *no*, it doesn't involve tights. What about you?'

'Well, that's a surprise.' She gave me a hug and headed off with her friends to class. Amanda had a surprise for me! Love was surely in the air.

With my head the size of Texas and feeling seven feet tall I walked off toward class. But before I could get very far, I bumped into none other than Warren Bailey and his loyal followers.

'Man like Superpants, you trying to get them digits aren't ya?' He leered and nodded towards Amanda who was disappearing in to the school building.

'No, we were just talking about the party.'

'Oh seen, who are you coming as then? Please tell me it doesn't involve tights. We all know what happened last year,' he nudged his nearest hanger on and they all smirked.

'No, it doesn't involve tights. I'm coming as Dracula if you must know.'

'Whaaaat! Man like Blacula yeah!'

This line seemed to impress his crew and they all laughed like a pack of hyenas.

'Why are you dressing up as Dracula, do they even have vampires in Africa?' This time the clan started high fiving each other like Warren had just made a free throw, but I had a solid comeback.

'They don't have vampires anywhere. Vampires don't exist.'

The laughter came to a halt and there were a few awkward looks amongst the clan as if they weren't sure what to do next. With his underlings beginning to show doubt in their leader, Warren saw the need to bring me down again.

'Yeah, well, I bet I can kick this ball higher than you.'

Kicking a football as high as you could was how we separated the boys from the men at our school. The aim of the game was to hit the ball on to the slanted roof that jutted out five storeys above our heads so it would roll right back down.

Not only was this close to impossible, you were more likely to break a window than hit the roof. So obviously the game was forbidden and punishable by immediate after school detention.

I knew I should just say no and walk away but I was desperate to wipe that smug grin off Warren's face.

'OK, let's do it.'

'Here, you go first.'

I took a good look at my target, cocked my foot back like a catapult and wham! Hit that baby as hard as I could. Luckily there was no smash of broken glass but it also didn't hit the roof – instead it flew straight through an open window. Warren and the clan immediately disappeared but it was like I was glued to the spot. Out popped Mr Davis's head, red and furious.

'Tobi Adenuga! To the headmistress's office. NOW!'

* * *

'You know I'm going to have to tell your parents about this,' Mrs Grisdale sighed as I stood up to leave her office.

'Can't you just kill me instead?'

She let out a small laugh. 'Go back to class Tobi. I'll see you at the Halloween party.'

Once my parents found out about this there would be no Halloween party. I might never see the outside world again.

* * *

'So apparently you are the leader of a gang.'

Remember when I said my parents love to exaggerate? One little ball gets kicked and all of a sudden I'm Pablo Escobar. My dad was clearly putting on show for my mum to make up for siding with me earlier in the day, and this performance was Oscar-worthy. Even my mum and sister Tola were impressed.

'I'm not in a gang, Dad. It was an accident and I didn't even break anything!'

'There will be no party for you tonight! You can go to your room, read your Bible and ask God to forgive you.'

Usually I'd give my parents a few hours to cool off, but time was of the essence. The party started at six sharp and I had already wasted half an hour on detention. If I was going to make it to the dance and repair my reputation, I'd have to plead my case now.

'Please, you have to let me go! You can ground me for the rest of the year. I'll wash plates, I'll clean the house. I'll even do Tola's chores.'

'You want to go to the party so you can regroup with your gang, abi?'

He was full Samuel L Jackson by this point.

'I'm not in a gang, Dad!'

'Tobi, don't argue with your father.'

'Let him go, guys,' my sister Tola chimed in. I noticed her eyes light up when I offered to do all her chores. Tola was studying to become a medical doctor, every Nigerian parent's dream, so it was no surprise she was the favourite. Having her on my side was essential.

'He's not a gang member Dad, trust me,' she looked at me and smirked. 'He was just standing up to a bully and made the wrong decision.'

My parents looked at each other like two Supreme Court judges deciding the fate of a defendant. I knew ultimately it was going to be down to my mum.

'OK. You can go, but there will be no trick or treating for you and you will be doing your sister's chores for the entire weekend. As well as all the washing up.'

Yassss! Party back on!

* * *

It took me a while to get ready, and since my dad was taking me to the dance I had to wait for him to finish watching the six o'clock news. It was torture. What if I missed the dance off, what if Amanda was falling in love with someone else right now? Finally it was done and he drove me to school.

'No misbehaving and I'll be here to pick you up at eight!' Dad shouted as I dashed straight for the school hall.

Pumpkins, cobwebs, bats hanging from the ceiling: the whole deal. I could see ghosts, witches, other vampires, even some Green Goblins (I really hoped they'd invested good money in their leotards).

'Hey Tobi! Surprise!' It was Amanda and her two besties Patricia and Ola. They wore identical black and emerald green dresses with hooped petticoats and hats to match. They even had their own personalised brooms to complete the look and the letters 'WHW' were stitched on each hat.

'What do you think?'

'You guys look amazing!'

'Thank you! We are the Witches of Hackney Wick,' Amanda replied with a slight curtsy.

'Man like Blacula yeah.' Yep, you guessed it, Warren Bailey. He was dressed as a werewolf, which was fitting considering his personality. If I was being totally honest, he did look good but I was never going to tell him that.

'You ready to lose this dance competition yeah? Man, if you thought

last year was embarrassing.' He shook his head, patted me on the back and walked off with his little puppies sneering and cackling behind him.

* * *

I had missed most of the warm-up games and all that was left was the fancy dress competition and the dance off.

The Witches of Hackney Wick won the Best Costume prize and rightly so. Then it was showtime – the moment I'd been waiting for all year, a chance to redeem myself and be crowned Best Dancer.

Warren was up before me. He danced to Backstreet Boys' 'Everybody' and basically mimicked all the moves from the music video if you ask me, but he got a pretty good score.

Then it was all eyes on me. I headed out to centre stage, got into my stance, and gave the DJ a nod.

Showtime.

And that's when things went left.

I was expecting the door creak from the 'Thriller' intro. What came through the speakers was the smooth sound of Swedish pop group ABBA. 'Dancing Queen'. This was not the song I asked him to queue.

Luckily the intro lasted an eternity, which gave me a few moments to think. I frantically tried to figure out how the DJ could play the wrong song. I thought about shouting for him to play 'Thriller' but my mouth was so dry at this point, I'd probably just let out a squeak.

It was at that very moment I caught a glimpse of Warren standing by the stage laughing with his clan of fools. He must have somehow switched my song. There was no time to think – I wasn't about to be humiliated for the second year in a row.

I channelled my inner dancing vampire and went full dance mode, doing all the moves Tola had shown me. I wasn't even sure if I was on beat, I just closed my eyes and kept going and by the time I opened them, to my surprise people were cheering and whooping.

Warren and his puppies couldn't believe it. To be honest, neither could I. I ended the dance by jumping high and dropping down into a perfect split holding my cape up high behind me.

As the song faded and I checked to see my church trousers were still intact (they were) the whole school broke into applause.

The rest of the night was a blur. The look on Warren's face when I was crowned winner was priceless. The judges said they had never seen anyone dance to ABBA like that. (They did look a bit confused but who cares – I won!)

My prize was a bright green skull that lit up at the press of a button.

I remember Amanda giving me the biggest hug before asking me to walk her to school the next day. I might have to listen to ABBA more often.

When my parents arrived to pick me up I could see cool dad had returned.

'You see, Best Dancer, Tolu! You know he gets it from me right? What's your prize? I hope they gave you money.'

Mum on the other hand completely lost it when she saw the skull.

'What kind of prize is this for a child? Do they not know we are Christians? This one is going in the bin, there will be no skeletons in my house.'

I just sat back and smiled. I had a walking date with Amanda in the morning. Nothing could ruin this night.

FAMILY IS FAMILY

DOREEN BAINGANA
CAMILLA SUCRE

Oh no. Here we go again. The family wants yet another grand reunion. It seems that whenever anyone – my uncle's wife's cousin or Dad's aunt's daughter – is coming home to Uganda to grace us with their foreign presence, the family wants a reunion. The question is, why do I have to join them?

I know what will happen: greetings upon greetings that take forever. Then the returnee with a fake whiney accent says, 'And who is this one . . . Ntambi? I last saw him when he was a tiny baby! Oh my, he has groooown.' The shock implies that they actually expected me to remain a baby for thirteen years. Then they pull me close into their tummy and try to suffocate me. The only good thing about being squashed in the warm, sweaty flesh is that my scowl is hidden. Apparently, I'm supposed to smile and enjoy being treated like an object, a stuffed animal or something.

And what am I supposed to do at these reunions? There's rarely anyone my age as all my cousins are much older, beyond university. What's worse, Mummy won't let me have my phone when we are with guests, saying: 'This is your chance to get to know your aunts, uncles, cousins: your people, Ntambi, your flesh and blood.'

I look down so she can't see me rolling my eyes.

'Family is important,' Mummy goes on, 'it's who you really are, isn't it, Daddy?'

He grunts in agreement and settles deeper into the couch and the football match on TV. He knows better than argue with Mum.

I can't help but try. 'My flesh and blood? *My* blood is the one that runs in my veins,' I insist.

'And how did you get here?'

'Mummy! Do you want me to explain? Ask Dad!' I'm now giggling.

Dad grunts, non-committal, his eyes not leaving the screen. 'Please take your arguments elsewhere; I can't hear the game.'

'Family is family', to quote one of Mummy's 'wise' sayings. The huge deal is Daddy's youngest brother is coming back to Uganda from Canada after nine years away. To meet him and his wife and kids and celebrate, we're all going to the farm for the weekend and we'll have a big lunch on Sunday. Dad is as calm as ever about this, perhaps because Mummy gets excited enough for the two of them. You would think it's *her* brother returning. She is moving up and down the house like hurricane, packing clothes and stuff enough for a month, making plans out loud, and chatting on her phone for hours. She seems to be inviting everyone who shares a teeny tiny drop of Dad's blood, which seems to be spread all over the town, country, continent and globe.

'By the way, Uncle Baku's two kids are coming. They must be teenagers by now, not so Daddy?'

He grunts, as usual. Sometimes I wonder if he proposed to Mummy with a grunt.

'Anyway, this time, Ntambi, you'll have company!' she says. 'You like to complain about there being no one your age at family things.'

Oh, great, so now I will have to deal with *teenagers*. Moreover, teenagers from abroad. Won't they be show-offs? Ugh! Tyree and Tyrone; what kind of names are those? Their mother is Canadian, so with their Nickelodeon accents, they'll probably say I speak funny and laugh at me. And of course, they'll have cooler clothes, the latest sneakers, fancy hair styles that Mummy won't let me have. What I want is never to cut my hair, never comb it, just let it be . . . shaggy, you know? Tell Mummy that and she uses this line like a sword: 'I'm your parent and I make the rules.' End of discussion. Talk about dictatorship.

Oh, and the farm? Two words: no TV. What's worse: the internet service is as slow as a snail. How am I expected to survive?

The farm is where Shwenkuru and Kaaka live. That's my grandfather and grandmother who are about one hundred years old and totter around looking for misplaced walking sticks and thick spectacles and forgotten cups of tea. They both break into gales of laughter at my bad Runyankore accent and repeat my mistakes over and over. I suppose with no TV, this is the best entertainment they can get. They should pay me.

My dad's oldest brother, Uncle Tofa, manages the farm and lives there with his family. His kids are grown and off at university or working. What can I say about the farm? All the mud in the world ends up in its valleys. When you smell cow poo, smoke and tobacco, you know you've arrived. Roosters scream as early as they can, so I wake up in fright at 6 a.m.

The first thing that hits when you enter the house is an ancient musty smell: the smell of the village, the smell of the past. It gets stronger as I am enfolded in my grandma's flowing robes. The old house has many dark rooms and cold corridors, and the sitting room walls are lined with fading photos of my grandparents, their siblings and friends. They were both teachers when they were younger, so he poses proudly by a Volkswagen Beetle, while she is small and springy in a mini-dress and a huge box-like afro! That photo makes me giggle. I can't believe they are the same wrinkly, slow-moving, absent-minded creatures.

* * *

OK, I admit there is something fresh about the farm. First, I'm just so glad to get out of the car and stretch my legs after hours cramped in the back seat. Second, the sky is so big and wide and the breeze so cool, like it's the first day ever. Third, Kaaka comes out of the house with the widest grin, and I can't help but smile back, even as I brace myself to be smothered in her swathes of smoky-smelling *kitenge* robes. Her greeting lasts for minutes as she hugs and shakes me, holds me at arms' length and looks at me in wonder, then pulls me into her chest again and gurgles with laughter. I can't help but return her warm hug. She lets me go just before I suffocate, lunges at Mummy and the hugging show continues.

The Canadians, who drove straight from the airport, have already arrived. The grown-ups get more intensely into the hugging, shouting and screaming, the slapping of backs and asking three or four times the same things.

'You're here? You arrived? Eeeeh! Welcome. How was the journey? Long time! You're well? You're good? Is it you really? You haven't changed.' or 'Look at you: you've changed!'

Meanwhile, Tyrone, Tyree and I eye each other warily from a distance. My mother is quick to see us kids mentally circling each other. She bustles over, shouting: 'Boys, boys, don't be shy, come on! Ntambi has been dying to meet you!'

I shrink, horrified. How embarrassing! When did I say that? Now I look like a desperate fool. I shrug, put my hands in my pockets and look away at the hills. Mummy pushes us into a hug. 'You teenagers bang shoulders or something these days, don't you?'

I want to sink into the muddy grass and disappear. I make a mental note to tell Mum when we're alone *never* to try to make friends for me or tell silly jokes at my expense. I peek at the boys, who seem equally embarrassed, looking down at their fancy multicoloured sneakers.

Teatime saves us from forcing conversation. The farm's milky tea always tastes richer, sweeter, than the usual one at home in town, as do the small bananas and hot plump *kabalagala*. Tyree points at them: 'What are these?'

'A kind of pancake,' I explain, feeling more confident now; I know a lot that's so basic that they don't, ha! They gobble up like six each. 'You're going to be running to the toilet soon if you don't stop,' I tease.

After tea, Uncle Topher suggests we take a walk around the farm. Mummy jumps in with, 'Yes, let's *all* go,' looking at me with her army commander's stare. I know any excuse I have won't work.

Can you believe I enjoy it? The hills slope up and down endlessly like a green ocean and wind rustles through the banana leaves with a kind of rough music, and when it goes quiet, it's like the world has sighed with satisfaction. It's like being immersed in Nat Geo Wild, not just watching it.

The two boys and I straggle behind, and they ask me all sorts of questions:

'Do you come here every weekend? Why not? How do you say chicken in Runyankore? And goat, cow, pig, tree?' Now I'm the expert.

They can't even say, 'Runyankore' right, and it makes me twist and turn over with laughter. Tears blind me as I can't help but squeal, laughing, when, *plop*! My foot lands in something soft, gooey, dark green: a huge lump of cow dung! Ugh! Ugh! Now it's their turn to laugh, so hard they fall into each other and fall down.

Rubbing my sneaker into the grass over and over doesn't get it properly clean. Well, that ends the walk for us, and back to the house we trek, still giggling.

* * *

It's the big day today: the luncheon. More relatives will arrive later, and the mums and house help are fluttering around in the outside kitchen behind the main house. Typical of Mummy, she takes our phones all morning, saying we must enjoy the farm. Enjoy it by force? Really? But that's her.

So, I have no choice but to join the two boys who want to try milking the cows. Sitting below the cows' white and black humungous bodies facing the pinkish-grey udders swollen with milk is a bit scary, but the cows are calm and patient. Squeezing the elastic teats so white streams of warm milk shoot out into the bucket is kind of disgustingly pleasant and fleshy

and sticky and satisfying all at once. Next, Tyrone and Tyree want to try pounding groundnuts with a huge pestle and mortar.

'You guys,' I protest, 'That's girls' work!'

'Is eating just for girls too?' Mummy juts in, as if I had been speaking to her. 'You boys are such a good influence on Ntambi!' she grins.

I join in the pounding, and we turn it into a competition: who can pound the pestle hardest and longest? Isn't it annoying when work becomes fun and Mum is right?

Finally, she gives us our phones back and we take off to our room. I had downloaded some TikTok dances, and want to learn as much as I can from my cousins to show off at school. Our room has a big mirror, which is great for practice, and we go over five different songs together, again and again, till we've mastered them.

Mum comes to our door, watches, silent for once, and then starts clapping. 'Hey, you guys are good! I know what: you're going to dance for us this evening.'

'Noooooo,' we protest in unison, flopping to the floor and on the beds.

'Why not?'

'It's embarrassing,' Tyrone says.

'We're too old for that,' adds Tyree.

'*They're* too old; they won't enjoy our moves,' I scoff.

'Wrong, wrong and wrong.' She points at each of us in turn.

'OK, for a fee,' I say, wiping sweat from my face.

'Your fee is lunch,' Mummy laughs. 'Now you sweating beasts had better shower again; lunch is almost ready.'

* * *

We stuff ourselves silly at lunch, which is served on the veranda. It's funny how, among all the noise of talking, there comes a silence when everybody is chewing and all you hear is murmurs and burps and grunts of contentment, and, 'pass the salt, please?' I must say this again: village food is a hundred times tastier than town food. *Matooke* so yellow and soft and hot, spicy pilau with tender pieces of roast meat, a purple mountain of steamed yam and another yellow one of sweet potatoes and pumpkin, and chicken stew a succulent oily orange. My hands and teeth strip meat off bone hungrily like I'm a stone-age survivor. I even try the *eshabwe*, which I usually don't, and its white, smooth, cool and creamy tanginess goes so well with the hot food. I wish my tummy would never get full, but alas, it does. Any more and I'll burst.

All we can do afterwards is collapse on mats and pillows under the green shade of huge trees and watch the sky.

As the sun softens and our tummies feel normal again, Mummy calls out, 'Hey guys, it's showtime!' As if she too is Canadian.

'We're still too full!' I moan.

'But it's been three hours since lunch.'

'Guys, let's just get this over with,' Tyrone says, getting up and stretching.

The grown-ups are still sitting on the veranda, with lunch cleared and the table scattered with tea-pots, cups, glasses and all sorts of drinks that are making them jolly.

Music cued, we three form a row on the lawn facing the veranda. First, some basic moves: arms up and over, foot side and back, around turn, and again, clap, clap, twist and on and on. We get smoother and faster and soon it doesn't matter that we're being watched; we are flexible robots flowing through the music.

They cheer and clap. We do a second song, then a third, why stop? From the corner of my eye, I see Kaaka get up and shuffle over, holding up her long brightly-patterned *kitenge*. Is she joining us? Really? Oh, my goodness, she is!

Kaaka watches our feet carefully, then slowly starts moving with us. Mummy claps and we giggle and pause. Tyrone changes back to the first simpler tune and we all move together. Foot in front, then back, side, side, skip, clap, clap, and again with other foot, body roll, clap, and repeat . . .

and Kaaka follows along! She can keep up, imagine!

'Go, Kaaka! Go, Kaaka!' The others stand, chant and clap along.

Mummy comes over to join Kaaka, and then, to my shock, Daddy too, with a comical stride, and then all the aunties and uncles and cousins come over, forming rows and columns. They laugh at themselves as much as we laugh at them, but they try. Now we're a swaying and swooping, skipping and turning, jumping and giggling group of young and old, wide and flat, small, thin, plump, graceful or not, it doesn't matter.

Somehow, Kaaka and Shwenkuru turn to each other and switch to our Kinyankore traditional dance . . . to pop music! It actually works. Arms raised gracefully like our Ankole cow's long horns, doing some complicated quick foot work in between rhythmic jumps as hips sway along. Smoothly, everyone gets into it, stamping as though the grass needs punishing. We boys mix the traditional jumps with our TikTok moves and everyone copies us – we're the experts this time!

Who doesn't work up a sweat? We laugh and dance and keep on dancing, moving all around one another. Who knew that to swish and sway and dance with Mum and Dad and aunts and uncles and the grannies would be such fun? Our dancing shadows on the grass get longer and clumsier. I look around and the sun has turned orange and is colouring the clouds pink and violet, all the way down to the bottom of the sky. It is smiling gently at us as it sets slowly, satisfied.

INTO THE FUTURE

JEFFREY BOAKYE
TOMEKAH GEORGE

OK, so you might not believe me, and it feels a bit silly to say it now, but there was a time when actual people used to actually call each other 'black' and 'white'.

It's true.

Honestly.

Can you imagine?

People all over the world would refer to each other by labels based on different colours. Which meant that you had something called 'black' people, and something called 'white' people.

I know. Weird isn't it?

It was back in the days when there were still only about 8 billion people and all of them lived on one planet – Earth. Only a small handful of humans had ever even visited space. Back when there was only one internet and everyone still carried their mini-computers, or 'phones', in their pockets. And get this: they even had to plug their phones into a wall every few hours or they'd stop working!

It was a very strange time.

It was a time when the most important thing about you could be the colour of your skin. It's hard to believe now, but in many parts of the world 'the colour of your skin' really did affect everything about your life. It could affect the way you were treated, how you lived, what kind of job you could get. Everything.

Sometimes, being 'black' could end up being a matter of life and death. It might shock you to hear that throughout those early days of human history (after we discovered electricity but before we discovered how to travel at the speed of light), humans could end up fighting, hurting and even killing each other over what their skin looked like.

Of course, it's obvious to us now that humans have never been 'black' or 'white'. So it doesn't make sense to split them up in this way. If you look at us, our species has always been a whole spectrum of shades – too many colours to list, really. Even more colours than you can find in a rainbow. It's all about a substance with the chemical formula $C_{18}H_{10}N_2O_4$, known as melanin, which occurs naturally in our skin, at different levels of intensity.

So how did it happen?

It started about 400 years before the first internet was created, when very early humans (who didn't even have phones) started spreading about all over the planet. They would travel across water in vessels made out of dead trees. It was very clever.

Some of these humans were greedy. They were looking for natural resources to take for themselves. They wanted to control different parts of the planet that were split up into 'countries'. A country was a part of the land that was owned by a particular group of people. If you look at an old, flat map of Earth, you will notice lots of lines criss-crossing all over the place, and lots of names for the spaces in between. France. India. China.

Cameroon. Peru. There were hundreds of them.

As well as wanting to control different countries the greedy people – people from countries that had been made 'white' by racism – also wanted other humans to work for them, and they didn't want to pay them anything in return. Many of these forced workers had dark brown skin, because they came from the part of the planet that was most affected by Earth's sun.

They were called 'black', because 'black' was thought to be a bad colour. And this meant that 'black' people weren't as good as 'white' people, because 'white' was thought to be a good colour.

These categories were known as 'races'.

The practice of judging people according to these categories was called 'racism'.

It was a cruel way of looking at people. It allowed 'black' people (or anyone who wasn't 'white') to be treated worse than 'white' people and it carried on for hundreds of years.

In many 'white' parts of the world, 'black' people were often treated like less than human. They weren't allowed the same freedoms as 'white' people. They were denied the same opportunities. They were discriminated against. From the seventeenth century onwards, 'black' human beings were set up as totally inferior to 'white' ones.

And the labels stuck. Even as late as the twenty-first and twenty-second centuries, people all over the world were still calling each other 'black' and 'white'. Despite being such strange colour labels, it had become the normal way of talking about people with paler shade skin, and people with darker shade skin. Worse still, whiteness began to be seen as normal. Whiteness was so powerful, so dominant, that anything that wasn't 'white' was seen as naturally inferior.

The strangest part is that humans are all mixed up anyway. We all share the same genetic codes. And after hundreds and hundreds of years of travelling around the world and mixing, the concept of a pure 'race' was impossible. They didn't know this a long, long time ago, but by the time the first spacecraft had been successfully launched into Earth's solar system, we should have known better.

But while all this was going on, something else was happening too.

Along the way, 'black' people from lots of different places weren't actually destroyed by the label that they had been given. Despite all the unfair treatment and cruelty, they did what all humans do best: they survived, lived and grew.

People took pride in being 'black'. And as humans continued to spread around the planet more and more, blackness became something that all humans could celebrate.

We're lucky. Those labels don't matter any more. Nowadays, we know how small Earth was, and how silly it was to sort humanity into lots of different races. It sounds obvious today, but putting people into categories like this is like splitting us up based on the size of our feet or something. Yes, the damage has been done, and we'll never be able to undo what went wrong, but we've learned, finally, how to be better.

It took a long time. My grandparents used to tell me about their grandparents' parents who could remember a time when things were changing. When people started to say things like Black Lives Matter and really started to celebrate the great things that 'black' people could do – things that had been ignored for too long.

Now, it's hard to imagine what it must have been like living at a time when racism was such a common feature of life on Earth. How it must

have felt to wake up in a world where so much pain and trauma was caused by something as random as the amount of melanin in your skin. It's hard to imagine the anger that people must have felt when racism kept on happening, even as we made more and more technological discoveries that would take us out of the past, and into the future.

It's also hard to imagine how thrilling it must have been to see people making a stand against racism. Those people were pioneers – those brave individuals who decided that the whole human community, all of humanity really, could and should make racism a thing of the past. I wonder what it's like to live through such a time, to see the world changing in front of your very eyes.

I know that nowadays we have all sorts of technology that previous generations could not have imagined (can you even imagine what life would be like without a holotizer?), but, in an important sense, our distant ancestors had something even more special. They had hope. When they realised things had gone wrong with how we were treating each other, they did something about it. They started talking. They connected. They resisted.

So, I'm speaking to the past when I say 'thank you'. Thank you to every single person who turned hope into action: young or old, 'black' or 'white', or whatever other ancient label was used to describe them. Even though the damage had been done, and racism was built deeply into society, there were people who wanted to make a difference. Black people who fought back, inspiring whole generations to do the same. They were nothing like those greedy people I described earlier. They were better than the racist people. They were the good people. They made a difference. And they did a good job.

For all of us.

Ancestral Voices

TRISH COOKE
RAHANA DARIAH

I go to a place where my ancestors still sing in the warm breeze.
I do not see them but I hear them in the sound of a cat's miaowing,
the screech of a cock crowing,
the hollow sound of a bird's coo-cooing,

Coo ooo ooo coo ooo ooo

I hear my ancestors' whispers in the rustling leaves.
They call me with their soft melody.
Sing-singing
their song.

And when the rain falls,
I hear their cries hiss through the *clear* mist.
Their spirits rise from the wet earth,
of birth, fertility,
life, growth,
and call my name.
Welcoming me.

They feed me a rhythm that nourishes my soul,
and their song becomes my own,
making me whole.
I sing it to all who can hear,
leaving a residue of hope
in the air.

I know my ancestors are part of the reason I do what I do.
So even though I do not live in the land of my ancestors,
I know my ancestors live on
in me.

The most joyful place I know is the beautiful Caribbean island of Dominica, that is, the Commonwealth of Dominica. Dominica is a small, mountainous island between Guadeloupe and Martinique. It was originally called Waitukubuli, which means How Tall is Her Body in the indigenous language of Kalinago, because they say the shape of the island looks like a tall woman.

Everything about the place makes me SMILE! The warmth of the people, the French creole language, the tasty food, the comforting sunshine, the soothing sea, the sweet music, the dancing! Yes, especially the dancing.

My parents were born there and left in 1957 to come to England, where I was born.

I first went to Dominica when I was twenty-one years old. I went with my dad, who hadn't been back for nearly thirty years. We had a wonderful time together, eating and drinking and taking in the sunshine, swimming and dancing and sharing moments. I have lovely memories of meeting some of my family for the first time there, too.

Dominica isn't the only place I have roots. Though some records were lost in a fire, I am told that my paternal grandmother's mother is from Sierra Leone. After a recent ancestry DNA test I discovered I may also have roots in Ghana and Nigeria too. Wow! So many places in my DNA!

I was inspired to write this poem when I started to think about what brings me joy and Dominica's lush green landscape came to mind.

Nigerian Jollof

DAPO ADEOLA

Jollof rice is perhaps the most famous of West African dishes. Its delicious aroma, rich and vibrant colour and sublime and spicy flavour are enough to get any stomach rumbling in anticipation.

The mere mention of it in the vicinity of any group of West Africans is more than likely to spark a heated debate over which African country makes the best and why, often ending in verbal warfare between the Ghanaians and Nigerians in the group, with Nigerians swearing that we make the best Jollof known to man . . . even though its origins can be traced to Senegal and The Gambia (apologies to you lot). We're just boastful like that.

I've often suspected that the real reason people have a favourite dish is more than anything else down to a memory or a feeling, that can be evoked at the mere smell of it. Which brings us nicely to the start of this little story.

It all started back when I was just a young boy, a bit tall and gangly for my age with a rather BIG head, and an even bigger imagination hiding inside it.

At the age of four and half I was sent to live with my aunt who became my guardian, miles away from my siblings and parents. I was told it was best for me (whatever that meant) so I took it in my stride. I found myself in a place where I had to learn fast that children were expected to be seen and not heard, and I was expected to obey rules that changed on the whim of my guardian rather than to question or challenge them in any way.

Life went on like this for a few years. I had developed tried and tested techniques and strategies for the life I'd become accustomed to. I'd gotten so immersed and occupied with what was now routine that I'd actually stopped believing that there could be more to life than merely existing. Looking back on it now, I see how scarily close I'd come to forgetting how to dream. I had no idea I'd made myself smaller and I definitely didn't notice the wall that I'd built up around me to keep others out. It might have closed me off from making new connections but it felt safer.

Despite this I found small ways of escaping through the books and comics I read and minutes of television I managed to steal, watching cartoons while my guardian was occupied with other things. School was also a sanctuary of sorts where I got to do and learn lots of fun things and be around other children. At home I had to shrink and be invisible, but in school I was asked questions about things (well the class was asked, but I could pretend it was just me being asked).

One Saturday afternoon the doorbell rang. Dutifully, I made my way downstairs and looked through the peephole . . . but no one was there. I took another look and just about made out what looked like the top of a head of grey hairs. I opened the door to see a huge

smile worn by a short, elderly woman with a rather large suitcase and bag in tow. She looked like a small, Nigerian Mary Poppins. But instead of the shawl, hat and umbrella, she had on a well-worn cardigan.

'You must be Dapo,' she said through a smile that caused her eyes to almost disappear.

'Erm, hello, Aunty. Yeah I am.' My mind was racing. Who was she? Was this someone I was supposed to have known was coming? Was I about to get in trouble for not being prepared for her arrival? I stood there nervously for a few seconds, not really sure what to do.

'Well, aren't you going to invite me in?' She said with a slight chuckle.

'Yes Ma, of course.' I reached for her suitcase and stepped aside so she could enter.

'Where's your aunty?' I was about to answer but the thudding footsteps coming down the stairs announced the arrival of my guardian.

'Ah, Sis mi, welcome welcome,' she declared loudly as she stormed past me as if I wasn't there. She threw her arms around the little old lady in a very rarely seen warm greeting that she only held for people she actually respected (or was trying to impress). Who was this little elderly woman?

'Don't just stand there staring, take Aunty's things upstairs and make us both a cup of tea,' my guardian barked while waving me away. I rushed upstairs with the case, dropped it in the spare room and almost tripped over myself while trying to make it back quickly but quietly enough to eavesdrop halfway down the stairs and find out who this person was.

I couldn't make out what was being said as both women were alternating rapidly between Yoruba and English, so I went into the kitchen and made them cups of tea, hoping that serving them would allow me to listen unnoticed and find out who she was and what she was doing here in this soulless house of all places. It worked like a charm. I found out that she was my aunt's older cousin, which meant she was my first cousin once removed and she would be staying with us for a month. Great. One more person to avoid around the house . . . no doubt she'd already been told how much of a problem child I was.

Two weeks passed and I managed to avoid the new arrival as best I could. The rules for survival were simple: never let your name be called more than twice, only speak when spoken to, and be polite while asking no questions. Sure you'll sound like a robot, but you'll be safe.

But the old lady was persistent. She constantly asked me questions about what I was reading or watching, trying to make me open up. She almost caught me off guard a couple of times with her warmness . . . almost, but not quite. I was on to her. In just a couple more weeks she'd be gone and I could get back to my books and cartoons and avoiding the regular hazards I'd become accustomed to.

One afternoon while upstairs reading I heard her calling my name from the kitchen. I jumped into my joggers and bounded down the two flights of stairs, making it just in time before the third call of my name.

'Yes Ma!'

'I need your help with something.'

'OK Ma.'

'Do you know how to make Jollof?'

'No Ma.'

'Well, you can still help me out, I need a hand,' she said with a smile.

'OK Ma.'

'Grab me those onions and peppers.' I brought them over as she laid out the other necessary ingredients on the countertop.

She lined the vegetables up on the chopping board, reached for a sharp knife and proceeded to expertly chop them up before blending them into a perfect purée. The onions made my eyes water but I couldn't look away. I was mesmerised by the skills on display. She was so graceful and efficient and I was so totally absorbed in what I was watching that I failed to notice her occasionally glancing in my direction, and the smile that flashed on her face at my keen interest.

'Pass me that pot please and be careful – there's oil in it.'

She poured in the puréed blend and after a few minutes added the herbs and spices. The most delicious aroma began to fill the room. I closed my eyes and drew in a deep breath through my nose . . . wow, my stomach gave a loud and embarrassing grumble which snapped me out of my daydream. We both laughed and with that much needed release came a flood of questions I'd been asking in my head the whole time.

'Where did you learn to cut things like that?'

'Aren't you afraid you'll cut your fingers off?'

'Why only two peppers?'

'Why vegetable oil and not coconut oil?'

She answered as best as she could, all the while smiling as if she'd won something.

Finally the rice was ready to eat, but first we absolutely had to fry up some plantain to go with it. It would have been criminal not to. I fetched some plates, cutlery, a couple of trays and two bottles of Supermalt and together we made our way to the front room to eat. The TV was showing an

old episode of Agatha Christie's *Poirot*. I wasn't fussed about old shows like that but they were all she watched during her stay – and watching them with her was like watching them properly for the first time for me. We ate, drank and laughed at the overly dramatic plotlines and when the food was finished, we cleared up the plates and sat back down to watch more Saturday afternoon TV. It was nice to not feel the need to go upstairs to my room for once.

This became our routine for the remainder of her visit. We were thick as thieves all through, cooking together, eating together and laughing at private jokes that only we understood.

She asked me questions about my future,

'What do you want to do when you're older?'

'Where do you want to go?'

'Who do you want to be?'

These were questions that I'd never dared to ask myself out loud because I'd have had to find the answers to them all by myself and I had no idea where to start looking.

But she gave me the space to talk freely and dream out loud without thinking about whether any of it was achievable. I spoke about how much I loved reading and drawing and all the different things I'd read, I asked questions about family members I'd never met, my mum and siblings that I'd forgotten about over the years. And not only did she give me answers to my questions, but she also shared her own stories of the past, stories about raising my mum and helping to nurture my siblings. I don't know if she was aware but her stories allowed me to make a connection to the life I'd been separated from for so long, a connection that I wasn't even aware I needed at that point.

I was super sad when it was eventually time for her to leave. My stomach started to knot up at the thought of things going back to the way they were. She must have noticed this because she took me aside before she went.

'Don't be sad. I'll be visiting again to check in on you sooner than you think,' she said while smiling her huge smile. She gave me one of her warm hugs, got into the waiting cab and was gone.

Things went back to what had passed for normal pretty quickly, but something had changed for me. I didn't feel the need to hide from the world up in my room any more. My curiosity was wide awake now and my thirst for knowledge was right up there with it. For the first time in my young life I actually dared to dream that I could possibly have a future of my choosing. I still didn't know what that looked like exactly or how to get there, but this was a good start.

That odd but wonderful old lady, who now showed up on our doorstep almost annually, went on to become my adopted Nan.

I won't lie, I don't cook it as much as I'd like these days, but each time I make Jollof rice I'm instantly transported to a memory of that first visit many years ago. The very mention and smell of Jollof always reminds me of my Nan.

The way in which a wonderful dish like Jollof rice requires us to combine different ingredients to make it, is the same way I believe life can often provide us with the ingredients to make our own version of family out of those we come across on our journey through it. We just have to be open to the possibilities.

Nan's Jollof Rice

ROSALINE TELLA

DAPO ADEOLA

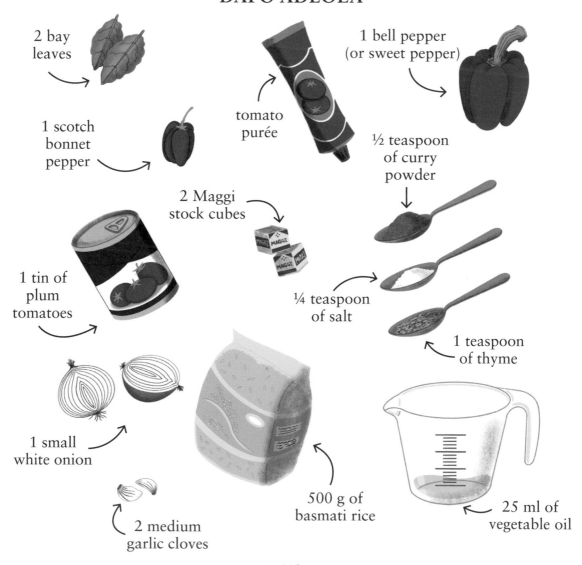

2 bay
leaves

1 bell pepper
(or sweet pepper)

tomato
purée

1 scotch
bonnet
pepper

½ teaspoon
of curry
powder

2 Maggi
stock cubes

1 tin of
plum
tomatoes

¼ teaspoon
of salt

1 teaspoon
of thyme

1 small
white onion

500 g of
basmati rice

25 ml of
vegetable oil

2 medium
garlic cloves

How to Make Jollof Rice (With the Help of an Adult)

1. Cut the onions and bell peppers into pieces. Place in a blender with the scotch bonnet peppers, garlic, plum tomatoes and 10 ml of water, then blend into a purée.

2. Pour the oil into a large non-stick pan and place on a medium heat for about five minutes, then pour in the blended tomatoes, peppers, garlic and tomato purée. Let it fry for about ten minutes.

3. Add the curry powder, bay leaves, Maggi cubes, thyme and the rest of the water, plus some salt to taste. Cook for ten to fifteen minutes.

4. Wash the basmati rice in a sieve then add to the pot and allow to cook for twenty to twenty-five minutes, stirring occasionally and topping up with water as required to stop it drying out or sticking to the pan.

When the rice is cooked through, serve with roast chicken, roast beef or fried plantain.

THE WAY HOME

MAAME BLUE

ROBYN SMITH

I've been dreaming about you. A lot. I miss you, I guess? But that's weird to say because you're still here, I know that.

In my dreams you're always singing, always playing some instrument and trying to get me to join in, but I never do. I feel bad about that. Even though in real life, you never made me feel bad if I didn't want to join in. Like, remember that time in Music in Year Nine, before everything got weird and Zoomy in Year Ten. I hadn't had breakfast all week and I came in grumpy, so you wrote that jingle on my keyboard to cheer me up? You just ran through the notes like they were nothing, picking a melody from the air, turning it into magic. All because you loved Cadbury's chocolate mini rolls and felt the urge to sing about it!

You were always funnier than everyone else. You're still the funniest, even now. What was the chorus again? Oh yeah.

It's a rock

It's a roll

It's the swirl to my chocolate soul.

Even when we met in Year Three, I knew you were a bit strange in the best way. You were also right about the chocolate rolls; I ate way too

many at your mum's after we heard the news. Can't really look at them now without feeling a bit sick. I know that would probably make you laugh too.

Now that I'm thinking about it, those chocolate rolls were definitely in my dream last night – we were in Music again, you only had one shoe on and there was a halo of chocolate rolls floating around your head like a . . . crown? Yeah, and you kept saying the same thing over and over again.

'Don't forget to feel joy, Anaïs. Don't forget about joy. Don't forget . . .'

I think I could hear your voice when I woke up, and it drowned out the shouting too, which was nice. I was trying to think of the last time you said that to me in real life, back when . . . when you were OK. Maybe we were at your house? I feel like that's right, because we were talking about gospel music – we'd found all these old dusty vinyls your mum had in the loft, by someone called Mavis Staples and another woman, Mahalia . . . Jackson?

Your mum let us use your nan's record player to play them and I'd never heard anything like it. Their voices were amazing, but the music felt so sad. I told you that, and you said that it was joyful too, that I shouldn't forget about joy. It was weird, because you said it like you were grown-up and you knew something I didn't, and you looked me dead in the eye and I couldn't tell if it was supposed to be a joke or not. I just know I haven't forgotten it since you said it.

It got me thinking I guess, and I've been writing more songs and stuff. That's why I came to see you today. Your mum said it was OK to come, to sit by your hospital bed and chat to you for a bit, that maybe hearing a familiar voice would help. You'd laugh if you saw what I was wearing right now though – head to toe in PPE, I look like a marshmallow mate! But you know, they wouldn't let me in otherwise. You'd probably tell me to take advantage of looking like I'm a doctor or something, that I should try sneaking into a surgery. It would gross me out but if I got to hear you laugh again, it would be worth it.

I miss you, you know? Even your crazy plans and the way you said 'vegebells' instead of vegetables because you know it always makes me crease up.

And I . . . I wish I'd told you sooner what was happening at home, how bad things had gotten. I didn't mean to disappear like that, but we weren't allowed to see each other in real life because it wasn't safe, and it was getting harder to get out of bed and I didn't have school to escape to any more . . . anyway I know we made up but then you got sick really fast so I never got a chance to properly say . . . I'm sorry.

I wasn't ignoring your messages, I just couldn't reply. I didn't want to share the bad feelings with you, and I knew that if I answered your WhatsApp vid, you'd know from my face that things ain't good and then . . . I don't know, maybe I thought it would break me? I didn't know you were breaking as well.

I'm really sorry.

And I wanna make it up to you, for real. So, I think I'm gonna be brave, for once. I know I said I'd never do it, that it was way too scary and not everyone is made for the stage like you but . . . your mum sent me this invite to an online talent show they're doing called Black Joy and it made me think of you. And I just thought, why not? I don't have to actually be on stage, I can just send a recording of myself, and your mum said I could film it in your bedroom. She even said I can stay over anytime I want, even though you're not there. I'm wondering if that will officially make me your stalker or not? You'll tell me when you wake up.

Anyway, the show's happening next week and just in case you're not up

yet to see me sweating on camera, I wanted to give you a sneak preview now.

Who knows, maybe you'll hear it and your breathing will be fixed

and you'll wake up, and we'll go back to yours and we'll sing together

and eat mini rolls.

It could happen, you never know.

Well, I'll press play now. I hope you like it.

Even in silence

When the signal is lost

When the rain has stopped pouring

And there's no road to cross

I'll remember your voice

Like a beacon of hope

Like the thing that saves me

My joyful way home.

The Book of You

DOROTHY KOOMSON
AWURADWOA AFFUL

I'm going to tell you a story
It's about The Book of You
I don't know if you'll believe it
But I promise that it's true.

At twelve I was shy. Really very quiet. I was also forgetful and clumsy, and loved to read and read.

I want to tell you about this particular book I once found. It was called *The Book of You*, and it was a book that changed my life. It might change yours, too.

✳ ✳ ✳

So, one day when I was twelve, I stood in the girls' changing room going through my PE bag over and over again because I couldn't find my plimsolls. They were black with black rubber soles and I couldn't find them anywhere. I felt sick. Really, really sick as my hand rummaged in and out of the bag. Our school was so strict about uniform, I was going to be in so much trouble. I might even get . . . a detention.

Detention was the worst thing in the world.

Detention!

When the teacher came to round us up to go out to the fields, I still hadn't found my plimsolls and I still didn't know what I was going to do. So I said nothing – I just followed the teacher and other girls outside wearing just my knee-length white socks.

I was shy, remember, and scared sick of detention, so I stood at the traffic lights with the other girls, waiting for the green man so we could get to the playing fields. The pavement was hard and bumpy under my feet. My heart was beating really fast in my chest. I didn't know what I was going to do, how I was going to play hockey on a field that was mostly muddy even in the middle of summer. All I knew was that I couldn't tell the teacher and it was possible she might not notice.

Just as we got to the edge of the field, 'Miss, Miss, Miss!' someone piped up. 'Dorothy's got no shoes on!'

The teacher, Miss Halliwell, stopped to look at my feet. All the other girls looked at my feet. And I looked at my feet, like this was the first time I'd ever seen the two things attached to my ankles.

The teacher frowned, like she was trying to work out if she was really seeing a girl without any shoes. All the while, my heart was going thudthudthudthudthudthudthud really fast in my ears. My teacher always acted like she was just plain old tired by everything – so she didn't bother to push her glasses back up if they slipped down her nose and she didn't bother to shout at the children, she just gave you detention and moved on.

'I'm not even going to ask,' she told me in her tired voice. 'Go back to school then go to see the Headmaster and tell him what you've done.'

I almost choked at those words because there was only one thing worse than detention: BEING SENT TO THE HEADMASTER!

✻ ✻ ✻

'Mr Moone is in a meeting right now,' the school secretary said, 'but you can wait in the library. He'll come and get you when he's free.'

She shut the door behind her and I sat down on the nearest chair. *What am I going to say?* I wondered. *What am I going to do?*

After I was sent to the Headmaster, my parents would be told. And then there'd be trouble!

Maybe I should run away, I thought. *I could—*

That line of thought was cut short by a huge book, which I'd never noticed before in the library, shooting off the shelves and landing with a THUD at my feet. The title was in beautiful gold lettering:

The Book of You

I was curious enough to move closer and peer at it when THUD! The book flipped itself open.

Yes, it opened itself!

At that point, I was ready to run for my life! What was this? A book that could open itself? Before I could move, though, the pages of the book rapidly flicked over until it stopped at the two blank pages in the middle of the book. I kept staring at the pages while I sat frozen in place. And then suddenly:

Hello, Dorothy, appeared on the right-hand page.

I blinked and blinked, wondering if I was imagining it.

My name disappeared and up came: **I know this might be a little scary** for you.

'A little scary?!' I replied.

All right, the book continued, **a lot scary. But there are few things I want to tell you that might help you.**

'Help me to do what?' I asked.

Help you feel better.

'Am I sick?'

Not that I know of. Do you feel sick?

'No, but you said you were going to make me feel better so I thought I'd better check. You are a talking book, after all. Although, technically, you're not talking, are you?'

I am talking in the way that I talk.

'I suppose so. Anyway, what is it that you're going to tell me?'

Oh, yes . . .

'This is a bit weird, isn't it? Me talking to a book like it's perfectly normal.'

No more or less normal than you almost playing hockey in just your socks.

'That was an accident.'

Forgetting your plimsolls was an accident. Not telling the teacher wasn't an accident.

'I didn't stay quiet on purpose. I just couldn't speak.'

Why?

'I just can't. Who wants to hear what I've got to say?'

You shouldn't say that, not when you're so special.

'Me?'

Yes, you.

'Why am I special and no one else?'

I didn't say no one else was special.

'You kind of implied it, though.'

I didn't.

'You did.'

I've never met anyone like you, Dorothy. Usually by this point, I've imparted my knowledge and the person who is reading me is feeling better.

'So you've done this with other people?'

Of course.

'But you're called *The Book of You*. And you said my name. I assumed that meant . . .'

I say the name of whoever picks me up. That person is the 'You'.

'Shouldn't that be clearer? Like, shouldn't you call yourself, *The Book of Whoever Happens To Be Picking It Up At That Point*?'

First, that's a ridiculously long title for any book. And secondly, no one else has ever had a problem with it.

'No one?'

No one. Most of them are just completely wowed that a book is speaking to them.

'Honestly, no one?'

No one.

'Wow. I'm surprised by that. I mean, really and truly surprised.'

More than the fact that a book is speaking to you?

'Books speak to me all the time. I've always made sense of life from books. I pick them up and they teach me about the world. They show me other people's lives. They give me the chance to be someone else. They allow me to understand other people. And that's how they speak to me.

I just always assume everyone experiences books like that.'

I think most people do but they don't realize it. Being able to see that is one of the reasons why you are special. You are unique and there is no one else out there like you.

'You say that like it's a good thing. It's not when you just want to be like everyone else.'

But you can't. You, like everyone else, were created as one of a kind.

'What about identical twins and triplets? They're created the same.'

They may look alike, but there is only ever one of each person. Identical twins don't even have the same fingerprints.

'Really? How do you know? Have they tested and compared every single fingerprint of everyone in the world?'

I doubt it, but it's a known thing that no two people have the same fingerprints.

'Wow, who knew?'

Going back to what I was saying: enjoy the fact that you are different. That there is no one else like you. *Revel* in the fact there is no one else out there like you.

'Ohhh, that italics bit was really cool. Do it again.'

No.

'Please? Please?'

Are you listening to what I'm telling you?

'Of course I am. As well as all that reading, I do a lot of listening. That's why I don't talk much. I'm usually listening.'

Good, because as well as explaining how special and unique you are, I need to tell you that there are times when you're going to be scared. You're not going to know where you fit in and you're going to be desperate to be 'normal'. But normal is what you are right now. Normal is what you will be in a few hours, a day, a month, a year, a decade, a lifetime. You are normal.

'Is that true?'

Yes. Every word. And you look amazing. Even when your hair doesn't feel right. When you think your clothes aren't the best match. When you think your face shape is all wrong, remember this: you look amazing. Your skin great. Your height is perfect. Your body is the right shape for you. Everything about you is right for you. No, you may not look like the people on the TV or magazines or any other part of the outside world and that is because you're not meant to. You are meant to look like YOU. There is no beauty standard that you need to live up – you are the beauty standard. You look amazing because you are amazing inside and out.

'Even if—'

Yes. Even then.

'But what about if—'

And then, too. We don't have much time left. Mr Moone will be here soon.

'I'd forgotten about Mr Moone.'

The last thing I need to tell you, is that you are luminescent, which means you are bright and shining and you light up everything around you. Everything is better with you around. Everything. Some people may say that you're annoying, some may act like they don't like you. That is a 'them' problem. You are going to meet people like that all over the world, all through your life. Don't take on their negativity. It's not yours, it's theirs.

'OK.'

And never, never forget that your very existence is a joy for all the world.

I heard footsteps approaching the library, and I knew Mr Moone would soon be asking me why I didn't speak up about forgetting my shoes.

'What do I say to Mr Moone?' I asked the Book in a whisper.

I don't know. I came to talk to you because you were about to make catastrophic mistake. Don't run away. If you're ever scared enough to want to run away, pick up a book first and remember what I've said.

'OK. I won't run away, I'll just tell him the truth. That I forgot and I was too scared to say anything.'

Good girl.

'Thank you, Book.'

I put *The Book of You* back on to its space on the shelf and sat down quickly before Mr Moone came in to talk to me.

* * *

How does this story end? Well I got lines for not speaking up and my mum and dad told me off. But it wasn't as bad as I thought it would be.

And obviously, no matter how hard I looked, I never saw that book again.

So that's my joyous story
Who knows how much is true
But all the nice things the Book said about me
Apply to you, too.

Best Laid Plans

TRACEY BAPTISTE
LEWIS JAMES

So the plan was to sneak out the back of the house, go through the garden, jump the fence, and then run down the hill to the Savannah. The plan was time sensitive. Not that anything in Trinidad really time sensitive, eh? Nobody ever pay attention to a watch in the history of this whole island. But I was to be there by a quarter of four, because Jasmine was going to be there by a quarter of four, and Jasmine never late no matter what. That was the only chance to get in. Jasmine's friend's uncle was one of the bassists in the Steel Teak pan group, and he was going to get us in the Savannah because neither of us had a ticket. As long as we were there to help take the pans inside.

Let me back up a little bit. I have money to buy a ticket, eh? Is just I can't buy a ticket because my grandmother doh like pan at all at all at all, and she wasn't going to buy any ticket for me to watch people beat pan. Not even for a legitimate competition.

'Pan!' she say. 'Pan? What you want to watch pan for?'

As if pan isn't the sweetest sound ever. As if pan don't make you want to swing your hips and twitch your shoulders and chuck your feet along the gravel.

Thing is, Grandma say there was a time when pan men an' dem was gangsters. Badjohns. They would have they pan sticks in they back pocket and a cutlass somewhere tie up under they pan, so when the fighting break out – and fighting would always break out – they was ready.

But Grandma don't realize them time long gone, and pan men respectable an' ting now. Pan men are not only pan men any more even. They throwing concerts, playing Mozart and Liszt and whatnot on the pans them. People going to these things dress up nice nice, and the conductor wearing a suit. So the days were over when a pan competition would end in police breaking up a fight, because whoever win and whoever lose, it was fight outside after. But Grandma cannot get her mind out of old-time thing.

Pang-a-lang-a-lang-bi-lang-bi-lang!

Well, competition start, and I still stuck inside this house. Is only five minutes I have to get down the hill.

'Gone dog!' I plead with Federal, the neighbour's rottweiler. I have never met a dog who don't like nobody like that dog. That dog real cantankerous. Plus, he's an escape artist. No matter what Mr Sooklal does, he gets out to terrorize the whole neighbourhood.

Four minutes to go. I could make it if I run. With Federal on my heels, I will definitely run fast. But Federal will for sure catch me and for sure bite a chunk out of my leg. So no. I need a new plan. And quick.

I check the fridge for something that might distract this menace of a hound. There's a big piece of cheese. It's stinky enough, I think. But still, I can't take my grandmother's whole cheese and waste it. I try to cut off a piece, but then it look uneven, so I try to cut on the other side, and then on the top to get it back in the shape it was before. It look good enough, I think, and now I have a few pieces for old Federal. Maybe if I throw them in different directions, it will distract him long enough.

When I get back to the door, that dog sitting there watching, like he waiting to see what I going to do next. Imagine. I throw one piece. The dog do a jumping sideways dive and catch that piece of cheese right in his mouth. Then he stand there looking at me like, what?

This dog not easy, yes?

I dangle the second piece, and Federal's ears perk up bright and his tongue lolling out his mouth. I toss it behind the mango tree, and he goes digging around back there, looking. I use the opportunity to run down the stairs. But before I even get halfway to the fence, Federal is there, licking his chops and looking at me like he's vex.

My heart beating. His throat growling.

I throw the third piece, and as soon as it release from my fingers I turn and run. I have no idea what happen to it, what Federal doing, nothing. All I know is to move like lightning.

I scramble over the brick wall, and I'm out in the street.

No time to catch my breath, I start running down the hill. Is a good thing I know all the shortcuts. I cut through Miss Basil's yard and duck under the wet clothes hanging on the clothesline. I scramble through the croton plants lining the Fords' house on the other side. I skirt around the chicken coop by Mechanic.

The whole time, pan ringing in my ears. Plim-pom-pang! Pangalangalangalang! Late! Late! Late! You miss your chance to get in the gate!

Watch me dodging people and cars like a boss running down this hill to get to the Savannah. Is like the music get caught up in my feet and they flying like notes in the air. Nothing can stop me. Nothing at all. Noth—

But where that car come from? A second before there was nothing on the road, and then bam, out of nowhere, this blue car come zipping up the hill. I was already out of the way, but I turn around when the tyres screech and see who else but Federal running at me, right into the path of that car.

Well the car stop. Federal yelp. I scream. The car driver come out to see if the dog damage. And meanwhile, Federal just standing there like a statue.

Who tell me to save this dog?

I run back to Federal and try to scoop him up, all thousand pounds of him. Well, I can't, of course. And he not moving.

'Get that dog out the road,' the driver say.

'The dog frighten,' I say.

The lady steups long and hard. She hit the horn. Federal still not moving.

'Come on, dog,' I say. 'You can't stand up here the whole day.'

Federal not going nowhere.

'Federal!'

Nothing.

Honk.

Nothing.

I pick up Federal's two front legs and try to pull him forward. That work. We go one inch. One more inch. Another. Another. The driver so impatient, she moving up as we moving aside. Like that going to make him go any faster. But finally I get him to the pavement and the two of we sit down on the hot concrete.

Pan ringing out so loud and so close now, I can almost feel the rhythm of it pounding out in my bones. But Federal still frighten and scooch up to me so close, I can feel him tremble.

'Right,' I say. 'Yuh good, eh?' I say. I get up and try to make the last few feet to the Savannah.

Federal have other ideas. He watch me and whine.

'Go home, dog,' I tell him.

He whine some more and take a few steps toward me.

'You can't come in the Savannah,' I tell him.

He doh care.

When I step, he step. When I stop, he stop.

I look down at the Savannah gate. I make out Jasmine in the crowd. The person next to her has to be the friend whose uncle was going to let us in. Her face looking round and round and every now and then she look down at her watch. I sigh. She look like she sigh too. The boy tap her on the shoulder, and the two of them turn toward the pans. I watch as they take up position by the frames and start to push the pans inside the Savannah.

That was supposed to be me. Right up inside the action. Touching the pans and them.

But no. I'm here on a dusty pavement babysitting a terrified dog.

I wait until the pans go inside, and two people close the gate behind them.

Well that's it. Opportunity lost.

'Come on, Federal,' I say. The dog wag his little stump of a tail and follow me close close close back up the hill. With every step, I feel like I'm dragging actual steel. Every note at my back is a sharp stab. I take him back to his own yard.

'Afternoon, Mr Sooklal!' I call out. 'Federal get outside again.'

'Again?' he asks as he sticks his head out the kitchen window. 'Dog? Why you so?'

I open the gate, let Federal inside, and close it behind him.

'He let you walk with him?' Mr Sooklal says.

I nod.

'You sure you have all your limbs?' he laughs.

I nod again. I too tired to participate in jokes.

I walk back to my own yard, and go back in the back way. Grandma is in the kitchen looking inside the fridge. She was not supposed to be back so soon.

'Girl, where you been?' she asks.

It dawns on me that Federal saved my behind. Because if she had come back and I was in the Savannah . . . 'Mr Sooklal's dog got out again,' I say.

She looks at me, surprised. 'You don't look like you missing any body parts.'

'He's not so bad,' I say.

'You know what happen to my cheese?' she asks.

I shake my head.

'Well anyhow,' she says. 'I have a surprise for you.'

I pull out a chair at the kitchen table and plop myself down.

'Mr Thomas is coming in a few minutes. He has extra tickets to the pan competition.'

My mouth drop open.

'You better hurry up and get ready. You not going anywhere sweaty and dusty like that.' She closes the fridge. 'I could have sworn the cheese was bigger than that when I left the house.' Then she looks at me. 'Girl, I say go and wash up. I thought you like pan. Sitting there with your mouth open like you catching flies. Ent you wanted to go? Is you who tell me that pan not like it used to be, not so?'

'I—'

'Let we go!'

I finally find my legs and stand up. 'Yes, Grandma!'

Sting Like a Butterfly

FARIDAH ÀBÍKÉ-ÍYÍMÍDÉ

KOFI OFOSU

If my life had a soundtrack, the first song would be 'Eye of the Tiger'.

It's the song that always plays in my head whenever a match is about to start. I feel this energy buzzing through me as I bounce on my toes. The referee hopping into the ring, the crowd screaming. Their eyes wide in anticipation as they watch me and my opponent, trying to guess who will win.

I suspect they never guess it'll be me.

They see my tiny arms and legs and assume I'm too weak, but do not know how strong I am from months of practise.

They see the pink of my hijab and assume that I'm too girly – when it's just my favourite colour and has nothing to do with how good I am.

They see my wide smile and think I must be too nice, but in reality it's a smile I wear because I know I'll win before the match even begins.

'In the right corner we have Sammy Gilford from Kingsdale School for Girls . . .' the announcer shouts, gesturing to my opponent.

Sammy is a tall girl with wide blue eyes, a mass of ginger curls and black and white boxing shorts matching her zebra print shirt. She towers over me and glowers, sending daggers my way with her eyes.

'And in the left corner we have Jazmine Mohammed from Baldwin Academy!'

The cheers aren't as loud. Like I said, people take one look and see someone who is easy to crush.

My favourite thing is proving them all wrong.

I hear Ms Yen cheering above everyone else. She's the teacher who supervises our boxing club – and the reason I even signed up for this match in the first place. I remember her showing me the competition poster a few weeks ago.

Junior Boxing Competition
Win a chance to train with a world-famous boxing trainer and an all expenses paid family holiday to Amsterdam!

Boxing is my favourite thing in the world. I practise all the time and I love spending hours watching boxing videos online. But I never thought I could be in an actual competition.

And now here I am. The semi-finals. I made it this far and I'm going to make it to the finals in London. I'm going to win and I'm going to make Ms Yen proud.

'Go Jazmine!' Ms Yen yells and I feel more energy rush through my body, making me vibrate in excitement.

The climax of 'Eye of the Tiger' rings in my ears as the referee begins counting down from ten.

I look around the room. So many people watching. Waiting.

Then I shut my eyes and I ask my hero for courage like I do before every match.

M. A. please let me be as brave as you. I want to win like you did. I want to show the whole world I can sting them too.

'Three!' the referee yells and my eyes flutter open. 'Two!' *You've got this, Jazmine,* I imagine M. A. saying back to me. 'One!'

Here we go.

I hold my fists up and I grin wider.

'GO!'

Sammy springs forward and I float away dodging her. When she stumbles I swing, hitting her square in the chest. People gasp as I punch again, this time an uppercut.

When I'm fighting, the whole world falls away. It's like a dance, and I am solely focused on my partner. With each hit, the crowd goes wild. The music in my head grows louder, the beat picks up and I bounce on my feet, dodging and punching.

Before I know it, the referee is holding my arm up. I'm sweating so much I can feel my shirt sticking to me. I'm breathing hard and smiling even harder.

I won.

I'm going to London.

'Jazmine! Jazmine! Jazmine!' Everyone screams.

I feel on top of the world.

But that only lasts a few moments, because the doors to the hall burst open. People turn towards them and the happiness I was feeling seconds before slowly dies.

I see my brother's sorry face as he marches in with my mum and dad behind him.

I step back as I see my mum's angry expression. I gulp.

And my last thought before I die is:

I am in so much trouble.

✳ ✳ ✳

There's something you should know . . . I haven't been completely honest.

On our drive back from Kingsdale, Mum and Dad are dead silent. Mum catches my eye in the rearview mirror, giving me her Watch When We Get Home Look.

This look can mean a lot of things. No ice cream for a whole week, my phone being taken away, or, worst of all . . . a stern telling off.

They'd let me collect my medal before dragging me out of there, marching towards Mum's Audi without a word.

My older brother Zafar hung back next to me as they walked on, whispering, 'I'm so sorry'.

I told him it was OK, even though I'm not so sure it is.

My brother is usually here at my matches, cheering me on. Sometimes he brings a huge poster with a gigantic drawing of me on it. Zaf's an artist. He's also my biggest supporter – next to Ms Yen. But Zaf couldn't make it today, because he had to be at parents' evening at our school with Mum and Dad. I'd told them I had an afterschool club, which they didn't question since I don't usually lie to them. Not until I started secretly boxing.

When we get home, I try to follow Zafar upstairs, hoping they will have miraculously forgotten about the whole being angry at me thing, and won't notice me slip away, but Mum quickly yells:

'Jazmine Mohammed!'

I sigh, knowing there is no escape.

Zafar touches my shoulder. 'It was nice knowing you, Jaz. When they bury you, can I have your room?' he asks.

I give him a death glare before heading back down the stairs and into the living room. Mum has her fingers on her forehead like she is trying to stop her head from exploding and Dad is sitting on the couch with his face scrunched up, looking very cross.

I swallow hard.

I already know what they are going to say – I've heard it all before.

'What in the world were you thinking, Jazmine?' Mum says, throwing her hands down. Here it comes . . .

'Do you know how dangerous this is? Girls shouldn't be doing that – sneaking off to fight. You're so small, they could have hurt you.'

'But they didn't—' I say, only to be cut off again.

'Alhamdulillah, they didn't,' Mum wipes her face. 'You got lucky this time.'

And all the other times.

'If I was a boy, would it be OK?' I ask.

Mum looks even more annoyed.

'That's not the point. You shouldn't be putting yourself at risk for a silly hobby. How long have you been doing this? If it wasn't for your brother we'd have no idea where you were. Do you understand how serious this is?'

I don't say anything.

If they came to my matches, maybe they'd get it, understand that I know what I'm doing and I'm good at it.

But I know they never would.

'Just promise me . . . us . . . that you won't ever do this again,' Mum says.

'Do what?' I ask, even though I know what she meant. She's made me promise not to box once before, when I first told her about wanting to join the boxing club.

'Boxing! Promise us you will never do it again. We don't mind you doing it at home with your brother, but not like this. Focus on school instead. There are so many other things out there that aren't dangerous, find something else, OK?' Mum asks looking tired.

I nod.

'OK,' I say. I've gotten way too good at lying. She looks relieved.

'Go to your room, I want to speak with your dad,' Mum says, and so I leave.

I've only just sat down when there's a knock.

Zaf steps into my room and closes the door behind him quietly. He's wearing our school uniform still, green jumper, and grey trousers. His hair is in corn rows this week instead of his usual afro and he's still got that sorry look on his face.

'How did it go?' he asks.

'They said I should stop fighting, even made me promise them again,' I say.

'Will you really stop?' he asks, eyebrows raised. I shake my head.

'Not a chance,' I tell him.

'Once they see you're as great as The Greatest, they won't think it's

too dangerous for you any more. They just need to see you in action,'
Zaf says.

I smile at that.

The Greatest was Muhammad Ali's nickname. M. A. = Muhammad Ali.
The greatest boxer who ever lived and part of the reason I love the sport so
much. When I was younger, we'd watch all his fights. Watch him effortlessly
swing his fists and defeat his opponents, time and time again.

He not only inspired me because he was amazing in the ring.

Muhammad Ali was Black and Muslim like me.

We also have the same name. My last name is Mohammed, and his first name is Muhammad. It's spelt kind of different, but you still say it the same.

'Thank you, Zaf,' I say.

'No problem, little sis,' he says.

He loves to emphasise the fact that he's older because even though he is in Year Nine and I'm in Year Eight, I'm the smarter one and he knows it.

'How did parents' evening go?' I ask.

'Let's just say I'm glad you took the spotlight tonight.'

'Zafar Mohammed!' Dad yells from downstairs. Zaf freezes.

'Pray for me,' he says as he leaves to face the music.

I think about how great I felt in that ring and then how upset Mum and Dad were. I bet if Zafar liked to box instead of play football or draw, they'd be OK with it.

The finals are in two weeks and I refuse to come so far only to miss them.

I need to prove to Mum and Dad that I am great.

No. Not great.

The Greatest.

* * *

Operation Get Mum and Dad On Board With Jazmine Being a Boxer and Fighting in the Final Match in Two Weeks

Zaf writes on the big whiteboard in his room.

I raise an eyebrow.

'That's a really long name,' I say.

Zaf looks offended. 'I personally think it is perfect, but fine – how about . . .'

He picks up his pen and crosses out the previous title.

~~Operation Get Mum and Dad On Board With Jazmine Being a Boxer and Fighting in the Final Match in Two Weeks~~
Operation Greatest

'I love it!' I say.

Zaf smiles, looking relieved. 'Operation Greatest, it is.'

'What now? How do we convince Mum and Dad to let me fight?' I ask.

'Well, it's simple really: Step One – we let them think that you have given up on boxing, and have instead found a brand-new interest – the spelling bee team—'

'Why would I join the spelling bee team, how is that going to help me with boxing?' He rolls his eyes.

'If you'd let me finish . . .'

Zaf pins a sketch of me at a spelling bee to the board and then next to that, a poster for the spelling bee in London, two weeks from now, the same weekend as the boxing finals.

Then he grabs another sketch, this time of me standing in the ring, with little Mum and Dad in the corner looking on.

'Step Two – give Mum and Dad the wrong information so instead of the spelling bee, they wind up at the boxing final, ready to see how amazing you are when you fight. I know that if they see you in action, there's no way they won't approve. Trust me.' Zaf really looks like he believes in this plan.

'What's Step Three?' I ask, still a little unsure. Zaf smiles and leans in close.

'You win.' He puts his hand out and raises an eyebrow. 'So, are you ready for Operation Greatest?'

Am I?

I can see so many things going wrong already. Like what if they don't like the idea of me being in a spelling bee either? Words can be rather violent after all.

Or worse . . . what if I don't win?

I look up at the poster of Muhammed Ali I have hanging in the centre of my room, from his famous 1964 match.

I can do this.

I put my hand on top of Zaf's.

'Operation Greatest is a go,' I say with a smile.

✳ ✳ ✳

I spend the next week pretending I no longer have any interest in boxing, but secretly spending every free moment I have practising with Zaf.

Just as Zaf predicted, Mum and Dad not only believed my lie about the spelling bee, they were so excited to hear me talk about something other than boxing.

I felt kind of bad, but I had no choice.

But something no one tells you about living a double life is how exhausting it is.

I go to school, I attend boxing club where I have to lie to Ms Yen about Mum and Dad's excitement, only to come home and have to lie to Mum and Dad about the joys of spelling. This evening at dinner, Dad excitedly pulls out the dictionary and begins testing me on really long, difficult words. Like 'commencement' and 'choreography' and 'onomatopoeia'.

I'm surprised they don't get suspicious, seeing how awful I am at spelling those words.

* * *

Later, when I get to my room, I do what I have done every day for the past few months. I turn off all the lights, climb into bed and open up my laptop, pulling up my saved videos of Muhammad Ali.

Tonight, I decide to watch his 1964 match against Sonny Liston. This is one of my favourites. I watch how Muhammad confidently swings, bouncing around the ring from one end to another.

Float like a butterfly, sting like a bee. That was his special saying. He said it before the match began, like magic words giving him the courage and strength to win. A mantra he probably repeated in his head over and over.

'Float like a butterfly, sting like a bee,' I imagine him thinking as he dodges and throws a powerful punch. 'Your hands can't hit what your eyes can't see.'

I think his special saying describes him perfectly. The way he moves in the ring, looking as graceful and as harmless as a butterfly. Fluttering about, his arms and legs springing as he backs away from his opponent. Then BAM – he strikes. Stinging like a bee. His punches are strong, knocking his opponents out.

Even when he's tired, he keeps stinging.

I hold my fists up like him and punch the air, copying his movements. Left, right, left, left, right.

Later, when I dream, I'm in the ring at the final. Everyone cheering as I float and sting.

Left, right, left, left, right.

✳ ✳ ✳

Wednesday
Three Days to the Final

Wednesday is the day that everything goes terribly wrong.

Time goes in slow motion as I bounce around the ring. I duck, dodging the punches of Penny Hughes – she's the best boxer in our school (after me of course).

Soon the practice match is over and Ms Yen is patting us both on the back.

'If you fight like that on Saturday, you'll definitely be walking away with that trophy—oh, hello, Mr Mohammed!'

The smile on my face falters. Mr . . . Mohammed?

I whip round, and standing there with a brown bag and an unreadable expression on his face is . . . my dad.

'So lovely to see you Mr Mohammed, I thought I saw you slip in a few minutes ago. I'm so glad you got to see your brilliant girl fight! She is going to be amazing at the final this weekend.'

I'm going to be sick.

I can already picture what will come next.

Dad will tell Mum that I lied.

Then Mum will yell JAZMINE MOHAMMED, and it will all be over.

All of mine and Zaf's plans, down the drain.

My dreams of making M. A. proud. Gone.

I feel my eyes water.

Dad stares at me unblinking, then he holds up the brown paper bag in his hands.

'I er . . . brought you some snacks, in case you got hungry. I knew that all this activity,' he gestures around the hall, 'would probably make you hungry.'

Wait . . . how did Dad know I'd be here?

'Th-thanks,' I say as he hands the bag to me.

Dad gives a small smile.

'I'll be outside. I'll drive you home, OK?' I nod slowly, then I watch as Dad smiles and nods at Ms Yen before disappearing through the sports hall doors.

* * *

After practice, I head over to Dad's car.

He's in the driver's seat eating chin chin and probably listening to an audiobook like he usually does.

I open the car door and the sound of the narrator's voice spills out into the open air.

I climb into the passenger seat and Dad turns off the noise and places

his bag of chin chin in one of the compartments.

Meanwhile I try and come up with an excuse, another lie, to save myself before it's too late.

'Jazmine—' Dad says, just as I'm saying, 'Dad—'

'You go first,' he says.

I breathe out.

Here we go.

'I'm sorry I lied about quitting the boxing team and I'm also sorry about the spelling bee. I know that when we get home, you're going to tell Mum the truth, but I just wanted you to know that while I'm sorry for lying, I'm not sorry that I didn't quit boxing,' I say, trying to sound more confident than I feel inside.

There's a long pause and I feel the urge to speak again and defend my honour but before I can, Dad starts.

'Well, I'm sorry too,' Dad finally says, which shocks me. I thought that he'd give me the silent treatment, or tell me how disappointed he is.

I suddenly feel like I've stepped into an alternate reality.

'We should have never said that girls shouldn't box – you're just so small. But that shouldn't matter. I knew how much it meant to you, I see how much work you put in at home with your brother and, well, when you told me about the spelling bee, I knew it had to be a lie. I couldn't see that sparkle in your eye you get with boxing, but also you and your brother aren't as subtle as you might think you are,' Dad says with a smile. 'I should have known when you asked for a Muhammad Ali poster for your sixth birthday that this wasn't something that was just going to go away. And today . . . seeing you box . . .' Dad has glassy eyes, like he's about to cry. 'Jazmine, you were born to do this.'

I smile at him.

'What about Mum?' I ask.

Dad waves his hand.

'She knows too. As I said, you're both pretty bad liars. She isn't 100% on board, but she wants you to be happy. I know if she sees you fight on Saturday, she will feel the same as me.'

'Thank you, Dad,' I say, giving him a hug.

'Oh, and one more thing . . .' Dad says, reaching towards the back of the car, and pulling out a box wrapped with gold wrapping paper and a golden bow.

'Here's an early thirteenth birthday present,' he says.

I rip open the wrapping paper and the lid. I gasp when I see what's inside.

Yellow boxing shorts with pink butterflies and little bumble bees.

I feel the tears from earlier start to flow.

'I love it,' I say. 'Thank you so much!'

'Every champion needs their winning uniform and I thought this would be suitable – what is it Muhammad Ali always said? "Sting like a butterfly?"' I burst out laughing.

'It's "float like a butterfly, sting like a bee."'

'Ahh . . . close enough. Well, maybe it's time for something new.'

✳ ✳ ✳

Saturday
The Final

There are so many people in the crowd. And while they are not all here to see me, the most important people are.

I see Mum and Dad in the crowd, sitting and watching anxiously – both wearing an embarrassing t-shirt with my face on it.

I see Zaf next to them holding a giant poster that says 'GO JAZMINE!' in bold letters.

And I see Ms Yen jumping and cheering my name.

As the crowd screams, cheering for their favourite and the ref gets ready to do the countdown, I look up at the ceiling, through the skylight and I swear I see a cloud that looks just like M. A.

I smile at it, knowing that he's here with me.

'Eye of the Tiger' plays in my ears as I float from side to side and the ref blows his whistle . . .

And then I fly.

* * *

It has been a few weeks since the final.

You're probably wondering what happened that day.

Well, here's how it went: the boxers from the other schools? They were bigger and better than anyone I'd ever fought before.

It was a difficult fight, probably the hardest fight of my entire life.

But did I win?

* * *

'JAZMINE MOHAMMED!!! We're going to be late for our flight!' Mum yells.

'I'm coming!' I shout just as Zaf bounds into my room.

He's excited about visiting the Van Gogh museum when we land in Amsterdam – Van Gogh is his favourite artist of all time.

'Mum says the cab is going to be here in a minute,' he says.

'Tell her I'm coming, I just need to do one more thing before we leave,' I say, smiling at him.

He nods, pats my head and then skips out of my bedroom.

I zip up my suitcase and pull on my trainers.

Before I leave, I look up at my poster of Muhammad Ali and the gold medal from the finals with 'Winner, Jazmine Mohammed' inscribed on it, and next to that an illustration Zaf drew of me looking triumphant wearing the boxing shorts Dad got me, with the words I yelled at the end of the match written across the top.

'STING LIKE A BUTTERFLY!'

Chasing Joy

HANNAH LEE

KEN WILSON-MAX

Sienna Slayter was the biggest movie star in the world. By the age of eleven she'd been featured on the covers of both *Vogue* and *Rogue* magazine, starred in over sixty movies and had a species of spider (*Aptostichus Sienna Slayteri*) named after her. But still there was something missing.

Like every other morning this month, Sienna had woken up before her 5 a.m. alarm to get ready to go to set. A lot of people thought that someone as famous as Sienna would get to do whatever she wanted, but Sienna had a reputation for following the rules, even when things got difficult. Yesterday, she'd filmed the same scene over and over again, saying her lines in slightly different ways until her voice cracked, only for the director to say,

'Actually, I think we got it fifty takes ago.'

It wasn't easy remembering lines, studying with a tutor instead of at school with other kids, and not being able to go to the supermarket without getting swarmed by fans.

Sienna sighed and stared out the window of her trailer at the children in the playground across from the movie set. They were practising a complicated-looking dance routine and even when they stumbled or forgot steps, it still looked like they were having the best time.

Soon her minder Jayne would come and get her to shoot a scene in her latest movie, *Joy to the World*, a story about a mischievous girl named Joy who takes a day off school and ends up having a series of wild adventures.

Sienna was nothing like Joy, but for a split second she wondered what life would be like if she were. She found herself excited by the thought. Sienna loved acting because she got the chance to see life through someone else's eyes. What if she went about her day seeing everything through Joy's eyes? She grabbed her phone and made a list of all the adventures Joy went on in the movie.

Today she was going to find a way to do them all.

✳ ✳ ✳

'Sienna!' called Jayne. 'They're ready for you on set.'

What would Joy do? Sienna looked around and her eyes landed on a can of beans. Suddenly she had an idea.

'BLEEUURGH!'

Word spread around the set that Sienna Slayter was sick and would need a day off.

Sienna hadn't had many of those before, but luckily she had her list to guide her. She looked in the mirror to check the chunky canerows she wore when she was playing Joy, slipped on big heart-shaped sunglasses from the prop room, then skipped over to the playground.

Sienna was naturally very shy, but since she was pretending to be Joy, she found herself striding over to the two kids standing by the bench.

'Hi, I'm Joy.'

'I'm Sasha,' said the taller of the two. 'And this is my cousin—'

'Khadeeeeeja, the diiiiiiva!' Khadeeja flicked a braid off her shoulder.

'No one calls her that,' Sasha said with a roll of her eyes.

'They will once I'm rich and famous. I'll live in a big mansion, go to movie premieres and be besties with Sienna Slayter. You'll see.'

Sienna coughed and spluttered at the mention of her name then quickly asked, 'What are you doing?'

'Making TikToks with the dance to Khamari Scott's "Angel Bae",' said Khadeeja proudly. 'It's taken me ages to teach Sasha, so if you don't know it already then maybe sit this one out.'

Khadeeja turned back to the bench where her phone was perched and did a dramatic spin and kick.

'Or . . . maybe we could do something together,' suggested Sasha, seeing Sienna's face fall.

'Anyone got any ideas?'

'I've got a whole list . . .'

Sienna took out her phone.

'"Joy's Day of Fun",' read Khadeeja. '"Number one: skateboard down Dead Man's Hill". You do know why they call it Dead Man's Hill, right?'

'No?'

'Exactly, no one does, because anyone that's tried to find out ain't lived to tell the tale. And here you are saying you want to skateboard down it! You can't be serious.'

'Only one way to find out.'

* * *

'WOOOOOOOOOO!!! That was amazing. Wasn't that amazing?'

'Yeah, it was . . . OK,' shrugged Sienna. The slide down the hill had lasted less than thirty seconds, which was great because Sienna wasn't a fan of speed, or the wind in her face, or even skateboarding.

'In other words, Joy wasn't feeling it,' Sasha laughed. 'Maybe you'll like the next one better.'

But she didn't.

Indoor surfing in a superhero suit got wet and itchy very fast. It also didn't help that they went for lunch in an ice hotel afterwards. Sienna shivered through Sasha and Khadeeja's second helpings of ice cream and imagined herself at home, wrapped up in a warm duvet instead.

She was secretly glad when every shop they entered stopped them from doing number twenty-two, 'shopping spree on rollerblades.'

Climbing the tallest tree in the park had actually been quite fun,
until everyone got to the top and was too scared to climb down again. It
was in the firefighter's lift down to the ground that Sienna started to think
something was wrong with her. The more items they crossed off the list, the
more excited her new friends got, yet the more tired she felt.

It was exhausting being Joy.

'What's next?' Khadeeja asked excitedly.

'Let me check,' yawned Sienna, but before she could a hand covered her
phone screen.

'No! No more checking, no more list.'

'Sash, what are you doing?'

'I've been watching you all day Joy, and you know what I realized?'

That I'm actually tween movie star sensation Sienna Slayter?

Sienna held her breath as Sasha's eyes scanned her face.

'You don't want to do this stuff, so why are you doing it?'

Sienna sighed with relief, but then she thought about Sasha's question. Why was she doing all of this?

'I . . . because it's supposed to be fun, and I want to have fun.'

'But are you having fun though?'

Now Khadeeja was staring at her with the same worried look that Sasha had.

'OK, how about this: forget the list. Joy, what do you want to do?'

Sienna blinked. She couldn't remember anyone ever asking her that question before. She wasn't sure she even knew how to answer it until she heard herself saying, 'I want to take a hot bubble bath. I want to curl up in bed and watch a movie. I want to lie down and do nothing.'

'Well then,' Sasha smiled, 'sounds like you need a new list.'

Plantain Moi Moi

ADEJOKÉ 'JOKÉ' BAKARE

OJIMA ABALAKA

Plantain is a big part of West African food culture. I come from two different parts of Nigeria: my mum is from the east and my dad is from the west. One thing that connects both parts is plantain – it is used all over Nigeria for making fufu and other savoury dishes, and overripe plantain is used for making sweets.

The first time I ever had steamed plantain I was visiting my maternal grandad. I was about ten years old, and I remember he made a kind of chunky, spicy vegetable stew with dried fish and served it with plantain moi moi. It was delicious. It is such a happy memory for me, and when I think back I realize that almost all my memories of my grandad involve food.

The spicy broth we always had in the mornings, the grilled goat dish he makes when we go to visit.

On my father's side, my grandma used to make a spicy plantain snack named after the town where they lived – dodo Ikire (Ikire is the name of the town). My grandma used to make it and sell it and I have all these memories of pressing out plantain to help her prepare the dodo Ikire.

Now I have my own restaurant and I use plantain in so many different ways: we have made dodo Ikire, plantain moi moi, even fermented plantain ice cream! It just brings me so much joy. Since I started my own restaurant I have realized how much food connects us. Lots of people come here with Afro-Caribbean or South East Asian heritage and they comment on how familiar our dishes are, how like so many of the foods from their own childhoods, even if they might be called something different. With food we can celebrate our differences – and our similarities.

How to Make Plantain Moi Moi (With the Help of an Adult)

2 overripe plantain

100 g green plantain flour

1 tablespoon paprika

50 ml vegetable oil

½ an onion, chopped

½ teaspoon fish sauce

½ teaspoon Ehuru or calabash nutmeg (optional)

White pepper to taste

1. Cook the onion in a little vegetable oil on a medium heat for five to ten minutes, until soft and translucent.

2. Peel the plantain and cut into small cubes, about 1 cm.

3. Place plantain in a blender with the oil, onion, flour and paprika, then blend, or mash very thoroughly with a masher.

4. Season with the Ehuru (if using), fish sauce and white pepper. Taste the mixture and add more seasoning if needed.

5. Scoop into well-oiled ramekins or foil containers.

6. To steam on the hob: place the ramekins at the bottom of a large saucepan filled with 2 to 3 cm of water, then simmer with the lid on for forty-five minutes.

7. Check occasionally and add more hot water from the kettle if it is going dry.

8. When cooked, a knife inserted into the mixture should come out clean. Serve with sautéed green vegetables.

WEBJØRN'S SONG

NATHAN BRYON

JESS NASH

It was kinda peaceful when I was sinking lower and lower, probably because I knew there was nothing I could do. I tried swimming up to the surface but I didn't have enough breath to make it.

It was the first time I had ever heard proper silence. Usually I live with my headphones glued to my ears, bass turned up to the tippey top top! You might think it would creep me out but I kinda liked the silence for once.

Suddenly I heard a song. Not like any of the stuff in the charts and not like any song I whipped up on my beat machine aka dusty old hand-me-down laptop. It was more like a whistle. A super high pitched and elongated sound went through my body, making every hair on my body stand to attention. It was beautiful. I felt calm. It immediately became my favourite tune. I had never heard anything like it before. I opened my eyes to see where this song was coming from and I saw it. A big eye blinking, a giant white fin, a huge white tail.

Before I knew it, I was propelled out of the water and flyiiiiiiing up into the air. THUD! I landed on the damp grass. I was definitely going to have a few bruises in the morning.

I looked around frantically trying to see if anyone had seen what happened, but there was no one else near the fjord. I lay there trying to catch my breath.

Every sharp intake brought in more freezing cold air: it stung but I had never felt more alive. I saw the familiar northern lights dancing above and thought they'd never looked more beautiful.

Shivering, I tried to look into the water to see if I could see the friendly giant that saved my life, or even a shadow darting around, but there was nothing. The water was still, like nothing had happened. Just reflecting the glowing green sky.

Eventually I gave up looking, turned round and headed home.

✳ ✳ ✳

I've been bullied ever since I moved to this new school. I hate it here. I feel like the loneliest boy in the world or at least the loneliest boy in Tromsø – just me, my mum and my music. I hadn't been having a good time. But this was too far. How could they push me into a fjord? Did they know I couldn't swim? Did they care?

I walk through the freshly laid snow in my drenched school uniform, thinking my mum is going to be vex with a capital V. I can almost hear her screaming my name when she sees the state of my uniform. She just bought me a new one because of my growth spurt, but for once this wasn't my fault.

I get home and my mum is on the porch looking out for me. She doesn't scream or shout: I think she can see the sadness in my eyes, not to mention my blue lips. She wraps a blanket around me, sets me down in her armchair and makes my favourite hot chocolate (3.5 marshmallows and sprinkles). It's like she knows. I love my mum.

I tell her everything.

'I'm calling the police.'

'Mum, please! No! I will never live it down – I don't think they did it on purpose.'

'How did you even get out of the water? Did someone help you?'

'Sort of . . . but you won't believe me if I tell you.'

'Tell me!'

'It was Webjørn. I was saved by Webjørn the white whale.'

In the kindest way possible, my mum tells me not to be silly.

'Everyone knows Webjørn is a myth, just like anti-ageing cream. The fishermen made him up years and years ago to try and get tourists on their boats to make extra money. If there was a giant white whale swimming in the depths of our fjords people would know! Every time they have really looked for him they haven't found anything. He's like the Loch Ness monster, or Big Foot. Just a myth.

I dig my heels in.

'I have never ever lied to you, Mum! Well, apart from the time you asked who broke your wedding anniversary plate and I blamed the dog. But this is different! I saw Webjørn. He sang to me. He saved my life when I had no one else.' My mum doesn't say anything. She doesn't want to argue with me – she's just happy I'm home.

I go to my room. I can hear Mum on the phone for the rest of the evening, shouting and sighing, telling various aunties what those bullies did to me. I do what I always do to make myself feel better – I go into my own world.

I put my headphones on, connect to my beat machine and I lose myself in making sick beats, beats so sick not even a doctor could fix them. My head is bopping, my foot tapping! I love this feeling. When I was sinking in to that water I thought I would never be making beats again, and thanks to Webjørn the whale, here I am.

As I go to sleep that night all I can think is that I need to say thank you.

* * *

The next day at school I saw the boys who'd done it. Anders burst into tears. Magnus even hugged me. He looked like he hadn't slept. I don't think they'll bother me for a while.

First period is Music, with my favourite teacher, Mr Klopp. He's basically the only good thing about this place. He likes the music I make, even though all he listens to is classical. I want to go to a music college to be a music producer like Jae5 and make beats for the biggest rappers in the world. Mr Klopp reckons I'm good enough but everyone else thinks I should focus on something else. Something 'practical', real.

Borrrrrrrrrring! I'll show them.

It doesn't take long for me to tell Mr Klopp what happened.

'It was Webjørn the whale who saved me.' He looks shocked and he's quiet for a bit. Finally he says, 'When I was a boy, I was out at night looking at the stars and I saw a huge white whale that didn't look like any other, playing on its own. But nobody believed me.' I was going to say that I believed him, but Mr Klopp had a far-off look in his eyes like he was a kid again, remembering that moment, so I just let him carry on.

'Since then I've read a lot about Webjørn. Some people think he is the loneliest whale in the world, because he has a song that no other whale can hear. People don't know if he's the last of a species or just different, but his song is at a lower frequency than all the other whales. So Webjørn will always be alone.'

'But I heard his song!' I say excitedly. 'When I was under the water, I heard it.'

Mr Klopp just smiles.

After school I fly home on my bike. I'm on a mission. The next day is
Saturday. Mr Klopp lives down by the harbour so I let him know what I'm
planning: I send him an email – I'm not sure if he checks his school email at
the weekend but it's all I can do. I tell Mum to come with me too.

I'm usually snoozing by 10 p.m. but tonight I'm glued to my desk,
headphones on, tapping at my drum machine,
messing with the bass, twisting the treble.
This is the most important song I have
ever made.

* * *

Mr Klopp looks excited. My mum
looks curious but worried. I just
tell them to wait: I don't want
to explain anything. I Bluetooth
connect my phone to my big
portable speaker which I've wrapped
in my waterproof trousers and jacket.
I just pray it can stay dry long enough
to play my song and gently place it next to the water.
I'm hoping it's loud enough that Webjørn will be able to hear
even underwater.

I play the song I was up all night making. Mr Klopp and my mum
just look at each other, confused.

'Thorin, what are you doing?' My mum starts to say – but then . . .
a giant white shape is rising to the surface.

Webjørn!

A tail splash covers Mr Klopp in water – my mum manages to dodge it (which is lucky for the whale because she just got her hair done).

The song I stayed up all night making is playing out across the water. Webjørn is right there, just under the surface. It almost looks like he is dancing. High and low notes, all layered up and weaving together to create this haunting one-of-a-kind sound. It's as close as I could possibly get to the

sound I heard when I was in the water. I think even Jae5 would be proud of this beat.

After a few minutes Webjørn goes under – for a while we can see the whale swimming under the water and then he's gone.

Later Mr Klopp comes over to ours and Mum is making hot chocolate again. I'm not sure if I'll ever see Webjørn again, but I hope he feels a bit less alone now. I know I do.

THE SKIN I'M IN

MALORIE BLACKMAN
ODERA IGBOKWE

Check out this skin
The skin I'm in,
Its flecks of gold
Its many hues.

Check out the skin
This skin I'm in,
It's dark and rich
So old, it's news

For every scar,
For each new fear,
I take my hopes
And hold them near.
Clear.
Dear.

For every lash
For each hard frown,
I may stumble
But never stay down

Check out the skin
The skin I'm in,
Within it there's nothing
I can't do.

Check out this skin
This skin I'm in,
It's made of stars,
Dreams old and new.

For every slight
For each fresh scorn
A child in this beloved skin
Is born.

For every shock
For each ignore,
I grow stronger
Than before.

So in this skin
The skin I'm in,
I may lose
But you won't win.

There is one thing
I know for sure,
I couldn't love my skin
Any more.

Check out the luscious,

Beautiful,

Wonderful,

Amazing,

Gorgeous,

Skin I own.

It brings me JOY,

LIFE,

HEART,

and *HOME.*

THE OWNER OF THE STORY

MATILDA FEYIṢAYỌ IBINI
TERRENCE ADEGBENLE

Welcome, intrepid reader. I suppose you're trying to guess who I am. My name, well, I have lots of names – but you can call me Onitan (it's pronounced *Oh-nee-ton*). It's a Yoruba word that means the owner of the story.

I hope your day hasn't been too long or busy and you've had time to rest, put your feet up and have a cup of your favourite drink. If not, go and get one now. I'll wait. I'm used to waiting. Waiting for inspiration, waiting for the sun to appear in the sky and waiting for the inevitable alien contact (which I hear is just around the corner).

Ready? You should always be sat comfortably with a drink when reading. When our imaginations run wild they can get really sweaty so it's important to stay hydrated.

So what's this story about? Good question. Well, the short answer is, it's up to you.

Did you know that you are made of stories? Lots of them – you're a whole book. You contain more information than an encyclopaedia!

If you didn't know then I'm glad to be the one to tell you.

You have ancestors whose lives were made up of stories that cooked up to make *you*, meaning you are part of their story too. There are tons of stories woven into your DNA – how cool is that?

You have been living with all those stories inside you and so this is my invitation to you –

let
them
OUT!

How do you want to tell your story? You could write it down, you could draw pictures or take photos, or you can just use your voice.
You could record yourself on a phone or a PC or a tablet.

Whoever says there is only one way to tell a story is probably someone who has no imagination – and should not be trusted. The truth is, to tell a story:

+ You don't need permission
+ You don't need money.
+ You don't need a dictionary.
+ You don't even need a pen or a pencil.
+ You just need YOU!

Because *no one* can tell a story the way you can.

Before we begin to explore the infinite stories you contain, it's important we do a quick warm up. You know what they say, even the moon needs the day to warm up for its night shift.

Nod once.

Blink twice.

Wiggle your nose thrice.

Turn your head to the left. Turn your head to the right. Turn your head to the left again. Turn your head to the right again.

Stick your tongue in and out like a lizard.

Pretend you're taking a bite out of a massive apple, so open your mouth as wide as you can – it's a really massive apple. Make some crunching noises if you like.

Now take a deep breath in through your nose and hold for three seconds.

One organising octopus.

Two tigers tangoing.

Three turkeys taking turns in a table tennis tournament.

And breathe out slowly through your mouth.

Now.

Who is the main character in your story? Are they an animal or a dancer or a chef or a poet or a robot?

Or is this story about you? Is it about someone like you, but they have powers, or they're a bit taller, or they're a bit braver?

You can make a character who is older than you, younger than you, funnier or more serious than you, or exactly the same as you. I enjoy telling stories with disabled characters, characters who are siblings, characters who are Nigerian – because that's my background.

Let's do some digging and get to know who your character is.

+ How old are they?
+ How do they spend their time?
+ When were they last angry?
+ What is their biggest fear?
+ Who do they love? Who loves them?

- What's their favourite song?
- What is their deepest, darkest secret?
- Who is the most important friend in their life?
- What is something they want, that they don't have?
- What is their name?

Now let's get an idea of where they're from. Where do they live? It could be the same place that you're from or somewhere imaginary. What does the air smell like there? What do they see outside their window? What can they hear? What does the ground feel like? What is the climate like?

So now you have a character, and your character has a home.

What else makes a story?

Usually a character has a problem. This problem could be big or small. Are they looking for something – or someone? Are they going on a journey? Is your character trying to change something? Or save the world?

No good story is ever straightforward. So when your character tries to solve their problem they face an obstacle. What are some ways that things can go wrong? Think about the embarrassing or difficult things that have happened to you in your life and yet here you are reading this book.

Your character must find a way forward, just like you did. What do they do to overcome their problems? Once they have taken action, you have reached your ending. Is it a joyful ending or a sad ending or a weird ending?

OK. I have good news.

You are in charge now. I am Onitan, but *you* are the owner of *your* story.

You are the battery powering the character and the world you've created.

Think about what story *you* need now.

Do you need a story that's going to bring you joy? What would bring you joy right now? Someone telling you a joke? Being tickled? Someone tripping up? Or something unexpected like eating a cake that tastes like lemon and spaghetti?

Do you need a story with lots of action? Flying, racing, martial arts, swimming, running from dragons, fighting monsters made of cheese?

Do you need a story with some romance in it? I know, yuk, but some people like that stuff.

Do you need a story that starts off sad but then ends with joy?

Or do you need a story with all of the above?

Then you know what you must do.

Tell your story.

I dare you.

YOUR STORY

ABOUT THE CREATORS

Adejoké 'Joké' Bakare (she/her) is a chef who moved to the UK with her family from Nigeria in the early 2000s. In August 2020 she launched Chishuru, a restaurant in Brixton, South London, in the hopes of shining a light on West African cuisine. She loves cooking and seeing people enjoy the food she makes.

Alex Wheatle (he/him) spent most of his childhood in the Shirley Oaks children's home, where he spent many lonely hours reading comics like *The Beano*, *Whizzer and Chips* and *Shoot*. Growing up, his heroes were Pelé, Muhammad Ali, Viv Richards and Bruce Lee. He is a massive fan of reggae.

Photo © Alex Wheatle

Arantza Peña Popo (she/her) is an angsty Afro-Latinx comic artist, zinester, and animator based in California, United States. She enjoys making work surrounding queerness, coming-of-age narratives, and mental illness. She also regularly makes cartoons for the *New Yorker*. When she's not scribbling she's rollerskating to Mitski and walking her chunky dog, Shakira.

Ashley Evans (she/her) is an illustrator based in North Carolina, United States. Her favourite artist as a kid was Ezra Jack Keats and to this day she still loves fairy tales and folklore. She loves dancing with her daughter in their living room and her favourite food is pão de queijo.

Awuradwoa Afful (she/her) is a Ghanaian-Canadian artist and designer working in animation. She was born and raised in Toronto, Canada, and she has had a fascination with animation since she was a child.

Camilla Sucre (she/her) is a first generation Trinidadian-American illustrator with a passion for diverse narratives and stories. She loves developing new worlds and illustrating stories where possibilities are endless. Representation in the media is something Camilla has long been passionate about and her work reflects her dedication to telling inclusive stories.

Camryn Garrett (she/her) is a YA author whose novels *Full Disclosure* and *Off the Record* have received rave reviews from outlets such as *Entertainment Weekly*, *The Today Show* and the *Guardian*. You can find her on Twitter @dancingofpens, tweeting from a laptop named Stevie.

Photo © Louisa Wells

Charis JB (they/she) is a Black-Latinx illustrator and designer whose work focuses on representing Black and brown girls and women. Some of their clients include the *New Yorker*, Google, and Disney TV Animation. She enjoys a good cup of black coffee in the morning, and a siesta around two o'clock.

Dapo Adeola (he/him) is an illustrator, author and character designer who rocketed into the picture book world with his illustrator debut, *Look Up!*, written by Nathan Bryon, which won the Waterstones Children's Book Prize in 2020. His favourite food is Jollof rice.

Denzell Dankwah (he/him) is an illustrator from Northampton, UK who enjoys reading comic books and graphic novels. He made his illustration debut in 2021 with Merky Books. He draws digitally and a fun fact about Denzell is that he is colour-blind.

Photo © Satyam Ghelani

Dorcas Magbadelo (she/her) is a British-Nigerian illustrator, equally obsessed with drawing Black women and convincing her friends of the joys of daily doughnut consumption. When she's not illustrating, she can be found screaming off-key at a gig, or just screaming.

Doreen Baingana (she/her) was born and raised in Entebbe, Uganda, where she lives now. She has lived in Italy, the United States and Kenya. She has won many awards for her short stories. She loves to dance, swim, hike and most of all, to lose herself in books.

Dorothy Koomson (she/her) is an award-winning, global bestselling author and journalist whose books have been translated into more than thirty languages. She featured on the 2021 Powerlist as one of the most influential Black people in Britain and appeared in *GQ Style* as a Black British trailblazer. Dorothy lives in Brighton.

Photo © Naill Diarmid

Faridah Àbíké-Íyímídé (she/her) is the bestselling and award-winning author of *Ace of Spades*. She is an avid tea drinker, a collector of strange mugs and a graduate from a university in the Scottish Highlands where she studied English Literature.

Photo © Joy Oluboyega

Funmbi Omotayo (he/him) started doing stand-up comedy in 2004. Since then he has performed in different countries, made a few TV appearances and even flown first-class from Australia to Abu Dhabi. He is a massive 2Pac fan; his dream is to be on *Celebrity Mastermind* with 2Pac as his specialist subject.

Photo © @shotbybinzy

Hannah Lee (she/her) is an award-winning author from London. She loves travelling, bright colours and honey (it's likely that in a past life she was a bee). Comedy and romance are her favourite genres and she enjoys spending time with her family and friends and meeting fab readers.

Jeffrey Boakye (he/him) is an author, broadcaster and educator. He finds joy in food and has always felt connected to Ghanaian culture through dishes he ate growing up, and he loves music created by all corners of the black diaspora throughout history. His debut middle grade novel, *Kofi and the Rap Battle Summer*, is published by Faber Children's Books in 2023.

Photo © Fossca Photography

Jess Nash (she/her) is a British-born Ghanaian illustrator who has been drawing on bits of paper since 1992. She is the most joyful when she's eating lots of different types of food from other countries and laughing with her sisters.

Photo © Mike Palmer

Kelechi Okafor (she/her) is a Nigerian-born Londoner who acts, directs, writes and hosts an award-winning podcast known as *Say Your Mind*. She runs her own pole dance studio in Peckham, South London. Kelechi wears many hats, and the head those hats are stylishly perched upon is filled with incisive observations about society, culture and specifically Black womanhood.

Photo © Yellow Belly

Ken Wilson-Max (he/him) was born and raised in Zimbabwe. He lives in London but travels back to Zimbabwe often. He loves creating stories, especially the ones where he can show that people are more similar than different.

Photo © Ken Wilson-Max

Kofi Ofosu (he/him) is a freelance illustrator based in Accra, Ghana. He loves to design characters and tell stories about the worlds that they inhabit. His favourite genre of music is lo-fi and his favourite dish is Jollof.

Photo © Kofi Ofosu

Koleka Putuma (she/her) is an award-winning South African theatre practitioner, writer, and poet. In a parallel universe, she naps and eats snacks for a living.

Photo © Lindsey Appolis

Lewis James (he/him) is a designer by day, illustrator, and lover of all things magical by night. Drawing and telling stories has always been a passion of his. If he's not drawing, you will find him dancing to 90s pop music, making YouTube videos or reading anything by Diana Wynne Jones.

Photo © Lewis James

Maame Blue (she/her) is a Ghanaian-Londoner and author of the novel *Bad Love*. She loves listening to R&B and eating way too much popcorn, and she finds joy in travelling to very far places like Australia.

Photo © Sinéad Gosai

Malorie Blackman (she/her) (Children's Laureate 2013-2105) has written over seventy books for children and young adults, including the *Noughts and Crosses* series of novels, *Cloud Busting* and *Pig Heart Boy*. Malorie finds joy in her family and friends, forests, and fun activities.

Matilda Feyiṣayọ Ibini (she/her) is an award-winning-and-losing, bionic writer of Yoruba heritage from London. Matilda would like to thank her loving family, friends, carers and agent for supporting her wild dreams. She'd also like to thank Destiny's Child, Sailor Moon and the Sailor Scouts, Missy Elliot and Janelle Monáe for their constant inspiration.

Michael Kennedy (he/him) is a cartoonist and illustrator who lives in Birmingham, UK. He mostly spends his time working on cartoons, thinking about cartoons, reading cartoons, and walking around the local park. Sometimes he can be found listening/dancing to jazz, reggae or African music. He definitely has a sweet tooth; ginger beer is his favourite treat.

Nathan Bryon (he/him) is an award-winning writer and actor who has written for award-winning children's TV shows, such as *Swashbuckle*, *Apple Tree House* and the critically-acclaimed *Rastamouse*. What brings him joy is BOOM VIBES, seeing friends on a sunny day, when his girlfriend loves his cooking and his mum's laugh.

Photo © Tim Lane

Odera Igbokwe (they/them and he/him) is an illustrator and painter who explores storytelling through mythology and spirituality. Their work is a celebration of the power of the Black Queer imagination. Odera creates work that is deeply personal, soulful, and intersectional. They love dancing, snacking, and sketching with family and friends.

Photo © Odera Igbokwe

Ojima Abalaka (she/her) is a Nigerian illustrator who likes to play. She finds joy in food, rest, and beauty. She dreams of being a DJ someday.

Olu Oke (she/her) has been an illustrator and printmaker for over twenty years. She lives on a Dutch barge with her family and a fearless cat. When she was little she would peel wallpaper off the walls around her house and secretly draw behind it. Her full name, Oluyinka Adunola Omoyeni Oke, has the same number of syllables as supercalifragilisticexpialidocious!

Patrice Lawrence (she/her) is an award-winning author who writes stories for anyone who will pay attention. She grew up in an Italian and Trinidadian household filled with great food and interesting music. Her current playlist repeat is Lady Blackbird's 'Black Acid Soul', but true joy comes from Studio Ghibli soundtracks, Bruce Springsteen and Korean indie.

Rahana Dariah (she/her) is a London-based illustrator. She studied at the Cambridge School of Art. Her work is influenced by her experiences growing up as a British West Indian, and spending some time of her life in Saint Lucia. Her work is full of colour and world-building.

Robyn Smith (she/her) is a Jamaican cartoonist known for her mini-comic *The Saddest Angriest Black Girl in Town*, illustrating DC Comics' *Nubia: Real One* and *Wash Day Diaries*. She has an MFA from the Center for Cartoon Studies and has worked on comics for College Humor, Nike, and *The Nib*.

Rosaline Tella (she/her) is the definition of a matriarch, who makes a rather tasty dish of Jollof rice. A mother of four, grandmother of seven and nan of one author, she's well-loved and appreciated by her family. Rosaline is a retired professional caterer and care worker who can now add published author to her list of achievements with her joyous contribution to this book.

Sharna Jackson (she/her), President of the Pineapple Belongs on Pizza club, also writes books and games – mostly about art or murder. Before she was an author, she worked in museums and galleries and made apps. Sharna lives on a ship in Rotterdam, the Netherlands. She wishes she could sail, but she's too scared.
Photo © Joshua Fay

Snalo Ngcaba (she/her) is an artist from London and South Africa, currently based in Johannesburg. She is self-taught as she didn't complete her studies, but that didn't stop her from chasing her passion for art. She is inspired by life around her and her experiences as a Black woman. She's a huge fan of Afro-Surrealism.
Photo © Snalo Ngcaba

Terrence 'Tbo Art' Adegbenle (he/him) is a fine artist and illustrator hailing from Mitcham, South London. He has a passion for creating art that represents and connects with his community and his love of hip-hop music and comic books. His joy comes from seeing children enjoying his art.

Tomekah George (she/her) is an illustrator based in Sheffield, UK. Primarily working with a blend of colourful and textural layers, she finds inspiration from her Caribbean family and her Black and British upbringing.

Tracey Baptiste (she/her) knows how to have fun. Tree-climbing, sea-swimming, trapeze-swinging, carnival-dancing fun. She is also a *New York Times*-bestselling author, best known for middle grade novels like *The Jumbies* series, *Minecraft: The Crash*, and the picture books *Looking for a Jumbie* and *Because Claudette*. You can find her on Twitter @traceybaptiste.
Photo © Viscose Illusion

Trish Cooke (she/her) is an award-winning playwright, screenwriter and actress. She has always loved making up stories and has written for many TV shows including *Eastenders*, *Tweenies* and *Playdays*, for which she was also a presenter. She gets joy from the lush green landscape of Dominica as well as its food, music and dance.

Yasmin Joseph (she/her) is a London-based writer. Her debut play *J'Ouvert* was nominated for an *Evening Standard* Award and won the 2020 James Tait Black Prize For Drama. As a child Yasmin was inspired by the flowers on her mum's balcony; they proved that any space could be transformed and made magical.

Photo © Christopher Okocha

Zaïre Krieger (she/her) is a writer and she really loves dancing. She loves Asian, Italian and Surinamese food (cooked by her mum especially). She grew up around a lot of gospel music and jazz. She is not physically able to whistle but wishes she could!

Photo © Bete Photography